Tianna the Terrible

The Anika Scott Series

Tianna the
Terrible

Karen Rispin

Tyndale House Publishers, Inc.
Wheaton, Illinois

Library of Congress Cataloging-in-Publication Data

Rispin, Karen, date
  Tianna, the terrible / Karen Rispin.
      p.   cm. — (Anika Scott ; #2)
  Summary: When her family leaves Kenya for Canada because of her
father's illness, twelve-year-old Anika needs the help of her faith and her
missionary parents to deal with her troubled cousin.
    ISBN 0-8423-2031-8
  [1. Christian life—Fiction. 2. Cousins—Fiction. 3. Family problems—
Fiction.] I. Title. II. Series: Rispin, Karen, date-Anika Scott ; #2.
PZ7.R494Ti   1992
[Fic]—dc20   92-19294

Printed in the United States of America

99 98 97 96 95 94
 8   7   6   5   4   3   2

For my daughters, Jennifer and Jessica

Chapter One

~~~~~~~~~~~~~~~~~~~~~

"What!?"

My mother's voice came straight through the floorboards. She was almost screaming, but partly laughing, too.

I sat up to listen.

"Kevin, we can't go tomorrow," she was saying. "It's just impossible! A family can't dash halfway around the world on a day's notice."

Daddy said something, but he wasn't talking as loud. All I heard was the soft rumble of his voice.

I dumped my book and shot down the stairs. As I skidded into the living room, Daddy was finishing, "—special price we just can't afford to pass up."

"Tomorrow?" I interrupted. "We're going to the States tomorrow?"

"No, we're not," Daddy said. He looked tired and thin because he'd been so sick. He'd caught hepatitis (that's a disease you get from dirty water and stuff) at an African church leaders' training conference in Thika. Ever since then, he just seemed to get more and more tired. But his big grin right now made up for how tired he looked.

"But, you said—," I blurted, then stopped. I swallowed and continued. "I mean, we have to go to the States, right? We can't stay here in Kenya, because the hospitals don't have the right medical tests for you here. And I heard Mom say 'tomorrow'."

"We are not going to the United States of America tomorrow," Daddy insisted.

"Kevin, quit teasing her," Mom interrupted, then turned to me and said, "We're coing to Ganada."

"Ganada?" I asked, and then it clicked. "Oh, you mean Canada!"

Daddy and I were both laughing, and Mom looked irritated. Mom gets her words tangled up sometimes when she's in a hurry or upset.

"Tomorrow?" I asked again.

She spread out both hands and looked at Daddy, "So your father says. I still think it's impossible. We just can't pack up our entire household in twelve hours."

"I'm sure we'll have help," Daddy said.

Mom said, "Mmmm," but she didn't look convinced.

"Well, are we going tomorrow or not?" I asked again.

"Yes, we are. I've got the tickets," said Daddy. "You run and get Sandy. We've all got work to do."

As I ran out the door I could hear Mom telling Daddy that he should be resting, not working. I just shook my head. I couldn't believe we were really leaving.

We'd lived in Kenya all my life. Mom and Daddy are missionaries, and we live on a mission station near Machakos. The mission station is a big, loose circle of houses, and all the people who teach at the Bible school or work in the Christian Education office live in those houses. One of the families that lives close to us is the Stewart family. I glanced at their house—that was probably where Sandy, my ten-year-old sister, was. Sandy and Traci Stewart are best friends.

But I didn't head for the Stewarts' house. I just had to tell Lisa Barnes first. Lisa is the only other kid on the station who is my age. She hadn't been in Kenya very long, and I remembered how much I didn't like her when we first met. She hadn't been too crazy about me, either. I could still see the grossed-out look on her face when I showed her a chameleon. I mean, I love animals of all kinds, and I think chameleons are cool. Lisa, on the other hand, figured I was just trying to scare her off. For a while it seemed like we'd be enemies forever, but then we'd had a wild adventure together. . . .

I thought about that, and my fingers went to my forehead. The ridge of a scar under my bangs was still sore and lumpy from where a drunken fisherman had hit me with a pole. *That was some adventure,* I thought, grimacing.

It still made my head hurt when I thought about getting clobbered with that pole—but I guess it was worth it. After all, it was because of what Lisa and I went through that we finally became friends. In fact, she was my very best friend ever. Something else that adventure did was to finally make me quit rebelling about going to the States.

"Lisa!" I yelled as I burst into the Barneses' house. "Lisa! Where are you?"

I skidded around the corner of the hall and into her room. She was sitting on her bed with headphones on. She hadn't heard me, so she nearly jumped out of her skin when I grabbed the 'phones off her head.

"We're going tomorrow!"

"Already?" she said and then grinned. "At least your forehead is only pale green now, instead of purple."

My stomach got tight. "I thought it was almost OK now. Do I still look weird?"

She grinned even wider. "No weirder than normal."

I threw a pillow at her, then headed for the door. "I've got to find Sandy and get packed," I said over my shoulder. "I just wanted to tell you."

When I was almost out the door, Lisa said, "Wait, I'll help."

"Come up to our house," I yelled and kept going.

At the Stewarts' house, Sandy wouldn't believe me at first. Then Traci's parents started asking questions, so I told them to come over to our house too.

"That's right," Daddy explained to everybody. "Just before I walked into Menno Travel Agency today, a group of six canceled their charter tickets on a flight into Amsterdam. I was able to pick up four of their tickets for a very good price. We are going to have to pack up quickly and travel light."

"I know you need to get yourself all checked out, Kevin," boomed Uncle Joey. He's not my uncle, really. He's Lisa's dad, but MKs (that's short for missionary kids) call adults who they know really well 'Aunt' and 'Uncle'. Uncle Joey was OK, even if he did always talk too loud. "Where will you be getting your tests done?"

"We'll be staying in Calgary, Alberta, Canada, with Hazel's brother, Kurt Malcome," said Daddy. "He's recommended a doctor there."

Where? I thought. I could vaguely remember Uncle Kurt—we'd gone to visit him and his family once when I was seven. But I couldn't remember anything about "Kalgry," or whatever Daddy had called that place. I started to ask Mom, but she just shoved a suitcase at me and told me to pack up all of my clothes that were presentable.

Pretty soon half of the people on the station were over packing books and dishes and things into boxes for storage. Our house looked like a bomb had hit it! There were people everywhere, yelling across the house to ask what to do with this or that. Lisa and I were folding up my clothes and sticking them in a suitcase.

It was hard to think with all the noise, but I didn't mind—I didn't really want to think. I especially didn't want to think about how I'd fit in in North America, or about having to stay there forever if Daddy's medical tests came out wrong. . . .

My stomach hurt.

Lisa was folding up one of my old sweatshirts. I flopped a sweater over twice so it kind of looked folded. I couldn't remember ever being in Canada.

"Have you ever been to Canada, Lisa?" I asked.

"I've been in Vancouver a bunch of times with my dad," Lisa said. She held up my old blue shorts and said, "At least you'll be able to get some better clothes there."

I stopped dead and stared at her. Some of the kids at the mission's boarding school had nice stuff from North America, but lots of us didn't. "I'll look like a total geek over there, won't I?" I wailed. "A green-headed monster geek!"

Now my stomach felt like I'd swallowed a lead pancake.

"I never said that," Lisa said, and I could tell she was sorry she'd said anything. "The green bruise on your forehead hardly shows now. You'll be OK, really. Probably better than I'll be at boarding school for the first time." She made a face, then added, "Besides, like I said, you can get nice clothes now."

I frowned and thought, *I doubt it. You need money to do that.*

Mom made Sandy and me go to bed early. She tried to make Daddy do the same thing, but he wouldn't.

"I won't be able to sleep anyway with other people in the house packing," he said.

I stopped brushing my teeth to listen. Sandy was listening, too, and her eyes were wide and worried.

"Kevin, you know you've got to rest," Mom pleaded. Daddy didn't even answer. He'd been trying to rest because he had promised us that he would, but he just wasn't very good at staying in bed when there was stuff to do.

I crawled into bed, then lay there, staring at the ceiling and listening.

"You can leave all your furniture here, at least until you know the test results." Uncle Joey's voice boomed up through the floor. "If you do stay in North America, we can arrange to have it sold for you."

I stuck my pillow over my head to shut out the

voices. If we had to stay in the States, everything in my whole life up would be changed. I'd never sit in the gray rocking chair again, or climb the mango tree. I'd never get to eat another samosa, or watch another sunset over the Rift Valley, or read my favorite copy of the Mowgli Stories while sitting on the porch, or even talk Swahili. Everything—absolutely everything—was staying here.

My throat hurt and the back of my eyes stung. I swallowed hard. I didn't want Sandy to hear me crying, but I couldn't stop it. The salty taste of hot tears was in my mouth.

"Anika? Anika? Are you crying?" Sandy whispered.

I rolled over with a *thump* and didn't answer.

"I thought you decided it was OK to go to get Dad's tests done," she said. "It really is OK, you know."

"Don't you even care?" I blurted. "Our whole life is gone, and you say it's OK. Leave me alone!"

"Our life is not gone."

"Yes, it is. How do you know we're coming back? I bet you can't even take Roo. She won't fit in the suitcase." That was mean and I knew it. Roo was this sort of cross between a blanket and a stuffed kangaroo that Sandy never *ever* slept without.

"Mommmm!" Sandy yelled. "Mommm!"

"Shh!" I hissed, but it was too late.

"What is it, Sandy?" Mom said as she walked in. "I told you to get to sleep."

"Well, Anika started crying and then she said we're never never coming back to Kenya and that I had to leave Roo here!" Sandy said, all in a rush. I could tell she was scared.

"I did not!" I interrupted, "I just asked how you know we'll ever come back."

Mom sat down on the edge of my bed and stroked my head. Her hand felt cool. "You're right, Anika, we don't know. If you're worried, talk to God about it. He's always here to help." She was quiet for a minute, then she sighed. "I know it's not quiet in the house, and it's been a traumatic day, but we've got another big day tomorrow, so you two try to get to sleep now."

Mom kissed both of us, then she slowly shut the door behind her, making the square of light from the door narrow to a line and then disappear.

"It's going to be fun on the plane anyway . . . and seeing Aunt Doreen and Tianna and stuff," Sandy whispered. She sounded like she was trying to convince herself. When I didn't answer she added, "I don't remember what Uncle Kurt looks like, do you?"

"Yeah, sort of. He's kind of fat and really tall," I said. I really didn't remember him all that well. I knew

Tianna was almost the same age as me, but all that I really remembered even about her was that her room had seemed completely full of Barbie dolls and comic books.

The next morning I woke up with the sun shining in the window and the sound of ibises flying over the house. Every dawn the iridescent, goose-sized birds flew over calling, *"Ma'nga! Ma'nga!"*

I stretched and smiled—and then I remembered: this might be the last time I ever slept in this bed or heard the ibises in the morning.

I propped myself on my elbow and reached for my Bible like I do every morning. It dropped open kind of in the middle, and I read, "Jehovah himself is caring for you! He is your defender. He protects you day and night. . . . He keeps his eye upon you as you come and go and always guards you."

Wow! I thought, *that fits!* Then I saw that somebody had stuck a bookmark in my Bible, which was why it had opened there. *Probably Mom,* I thought, but I read the whole chapter, Psalm 121, over anyway. It really made me think. God was promising to look after us. . . . He said he is never sleeping and that he wouldn't let anything hurt us.

When I looked around, Sandy was sitting up looking at me. "You still scared?" she asked.

I just kind of grunted, and she said, "I'm not. It will be fun and—"

"OK! Everybody up!" Mom threw open our door. "Get dressed and let's get going. I want you to lay out dresses to wear to the airport."

"Mom! We can't!" I interrupted. "I hate all my dresses."

All Mom said was, "Let's not start the day by arguing. I want you downstairs in ten minutes."

The rest of that morning was like a strange dream. I wandered across the station by myself, touching things, saying good-bye. Things seemed closer and bigger than usual: the smell of frangipani, the feel of the bark on the jacaranda tree, the warmth of the strong golden sun on my shoulders, and the smell of the dry red dust. It was hard to pay attention to people at all.

"Anika!" Sandy yelled, "Anika!" She ran toward me through the Stewarts' yard. A shock went through me. What time was it?

"Boy, are you ever in trouble. The car's loaded, and everybody's looking for you," she yelled. "Come on!"

I raced after her, and Mom started scolding as soon as I hit the door. She followed me upstairs, still scolding. I yanked my dress on, but it was tight under the armpits so I jerked it down.

"Anika, you knew that dress was too small," Mom's voice drilled at me. "Don't you care how you look?"

"Hazel, Anika! Hurry up!" Daddy called.

Too small or not, the dress would have to do. I grabbed my carry-on case and ran downstairs, with Mom following right behind me. A few minutes later we were on our way.

The airport was like a blur. The loudspeakers were announcing flights in cool voices; everything smelled like cigarette smoke and jet fuel. After Daddy checked the luggage through, we boarded the plane, found our seats, and buckled in. I ended up with a window seat, sitting by Daddy. Sandy and Mom were in front of us. As we taxied, I watched the lion-colored grass that lined the runway. Then the engines screamed and the plane shuddered for a second. When the pilot took the brakes off we were pressed back into our seats, and then we were off.

Daddy's shoulder was heavy where he leaned up against me to watch the takeoff. He reached across me to point out the Aberdare mountains, then Mount Kenya, its snow shining in the bright sun. He likes to explain things all the time like he's a tour guide. Right now I just wished he would leave me alone. My throat was so tight I couldn't say anything at all. How could I ever fit in anywhere else when Kenya was so beautiful?

After a bit, Daddy stopped talking. I looked over at him. He had leaned back with his eyes closed; he looked so thin and tired. I turned back to the window and frowned.

Why did God have to let him get sick in the first place? I thought angrily.

I couldn't see anything now except the rough white tops of clouds. The plastic frame of the window felt cold, and the plane's vibrations ran right through my skull.

In spite of it, though, I must have gone to sleep. Next thing I knew, my head bumped the edge of the window hard and bounced. I sat up and put my hand on my temple where it hurt. The seatbelt sign went on with a *'bing'*.

"Ladies and gentlemen, this is your captain speaking," said a voice over the intercom. "Please fasten your seatbelts. We will be experiencing some turbulence over the Ethiopian highlands."

Still half-asleep, I found my seatbelt and latched it. Another hard bump shoved me forward against the seatbelt.

I looked at Daddy. He was putting his seatbelt on, but he didn't look scared at all.

"Don't worry," he said, smiling at me. "The pilots are very careful to stay out of weather that the plane isn't designed to handle. Now that you're awake, Anika, there's something I wanted to talk to you about." He sounded really serious. I gulped. Maybe he'd tell me that we were going to stay in Canada for sure, or maybe he'd say that he was going to die. I shoved those thoughts away and tried to listen.

Glancing at me, Daddy went on. "Mom and I don't usually talk to you kids about adult problems, but this time we felt we should."

He paused. I couldn't stand it if he decided not to tell me after all. I did my best to look grown-up and responsible, so he'd talk to me. But it's hard to look that way when you're being joggled all over by an airplane that seems to have the hiccups.

Finally, he said, "Mom's brother, Kurt, and his wife, Doreen, are having serious problems with their marriage."

I let my breath out. At least it wasn't about him or Mom.

"Your uncle Kurt made a commitment to Christ when he was a child, but from what he's told us he hasn't been living the way he should. As far as we know, Aunt Doreen doesn't know Christ. Kurt wrote us a letter asking us to come stay with them. He . . . he seems to be looking for help."

"You mean we're going to Calgary partly to try to help Uncle Kurt?" I asked.

"Well, I don't know how much *we* can help, but your

mother and I have been praying for Kurt and Doreen. And we know that the Lord can help with any situation." Daddy said. "When the need for this trip came up at the same time as Kurt's invitation, Mom and I felt it was something God had set up. But God won't be using just Mom and me. You and Sandy are important parts of what God wants to do, too. Kurt said he wanted to see how a Christian family worked." Daddy paused for a minute, then sighed. "I'm not sure what Kurt expects to see in our family. It could make me a little nervous, if I didn't know that the Lord was in this."

Oh great! I thought. *Now I not only have to try and fit into a place I've never been, but I'll have to do everything right so Uncle Kurt thinks Christians are good!*

Daddy glanced at me. I must have been looking worried, because he reached over to touch my cheek and smile. "Don't worry, Anika. I know we're not perfect—we make mistakes and we get frustrated with each other . . . but God never said we had to be perfect to be used. I just wanted to let you know a little of what's going on and to ask you just to be yourself. That's the best way you can help."

I thought for a minute about what Daddy had said. What would it be like to stay with people who were having marriage problems? Did they fight a lot? Were they mean to each other? I wondered what it was like for my cousin Tianna. I couldn't even imagine having Mom and Daddy mad at each other all the time.

I swallowed and said, "I can witness to Tianna, I guess."

"Be careful, Anika," Daddy said gently. "You tend to jump into situations and act without thinking. We'll have to proceed with a great deal of tact and even more prayer. In fact, why don't you and I pray together right now?"

"Can't I just pray in my head?" I asked. I felt confused inside, and I didn't want to try to pray out loud when I didn't know what I thought. Besides, what if a stewardess came?

"If that's what you want," Daddy said. He leaned back and shut his eyes.

I tried to pray for Uncle Kurt and Aunt Doreen, and especially for Tianna—but it's hard to pray for someone when all you remember about them is that their room used to be full of Barbie dolls and comic books. Worries about Daddy being sick and about how I'd fit in when we were in Canada kept getting in the way. It was like my brain was full of noise.

Then I got this idea that made it all make sense. I've never been able to be quiet about a good idea.

"Hey, I know," I said, sitting up straight and shaking Daddy's arm. "Probably God just wants us to go to Canada to help Uncle Kurt's family. After your tests are OK, and Uncle Kurt, Aunt Doreen, and Tianna all get to be Christians, we can just come back to Kenya."

Daddy laughed and said, "I wish everything was always that simple."

It made so much sense to me. I couldn't be wrong, could I?

Chapter Two

I looked up. The seatbelt sign was off, and I'd never even noticed when we'd quit bumping around.

"Anika," Mom said, standing up, "I'd like to sit with Daddy for a while, so I'll trade you seats."

I groaned, but obeyed. When I sat down, Sandy was looking out the window, and her head blocked the view.

"Hey, neat!" she said.

I ignored her. She was probably just trying to make me jealous that she had the window seat.

She looked over at me and said, "No, really. Look," and moved back so I could see.

I still ignored her.

Mom said, "Anika," in her warning voice. I sighed and leaned over to look.

The clouds were gone, and the land looked really weird. It was all tan and pale with wrinkled little brown hills or mountains, but right across the middle was this green strip that got wide and narrow. There was a smaller silvery brown strip wandering through the middle of the green one.

"That's the Nile River, girls," Daddy said very loudly in his tour-guide voice.

I looked around nervously, sure everyone was staring at us. When I turned back to our window, Sandy had stuck her head right in the middle of it again.

"Hey! Move back," I said.

"But I can't see if I back up."

"Well, don't cover up the whole window!" I said.

She didn't budge, so I shoved her. She shoved me right back.

"That's enough! How do you expect to act properly in front of Uncle Kurt and Aunt Doreen if you can't even get along now?" Daddy said. "Apologize to each other, and work together."

Sandy and I both muttered, "Sorry." She sort of half leaned back, so I could see out OK—not great, but OK. Daddy started tour guiding again. It was embarrassing.

I tried to pretend I was a sophisticated world traveler looking out at the Nile River. It's hard to do that, though, when you and your sister are having a secret shoving fight.

"Would you like a hot washcloth?" someone said right in my ear. I jumped. A stewardess was leaning over my seat with a pair of tongs holding a white wash-cloth. It was steaming.

"Um, I guess so," I stammered.

She dropped it in my hands, then smiled at Sandy and held another one out to her.

When the stewardess went on to Mom and Dad, Sandy and I just looked at each other, each of us sitting there holding the hot washcloths. We both burst out giggling.

Sandy held hers up by one corner and looked at it like it was an unknown species of animal, and we both cracked up all over again.

Something bumped my arm, and I looked up. It was the woman from across the aisle. I'd noticed her before. She was sort of old, but looked rich and pretty.

"To wash with, no?" she said with a French accent, and pointed in a graceful, lazy way with her whole hand at my washcloth.

I managed to thank her.

"You have such nice family," she said with a smile. "I have much enjoy watching you."

I stammered a thank-you again. She nodded her head gracefully, then turned and picked up her own washcloth.

"She must think we're really stupid," Sandy whispered as she rubbed her hands on her washcloth.

I nodded. The woman across the aisle obviously was a sophisticated world traveler. She'd never be afraid of going to Canada.

"'To wash with, no?'" Sandy imitated in a whisper, and made a dainty swipe at her cheek, then looked past me with one eyebrow up. I followed her glance, and cracked up completely.

The lady was delicately patting one of her eyebrows with her cloth. Her eyes were elegantly shut.

I tried it, half in fun, half to practice being elegant. The washcloth felt so good on my face that I gave up elegance and buried my face in it. It was super to get rid of some of the itchy, stale feeling.

When I looked up, the woman across the aisle was watching me with a twinkle in her eye. I wasn't sure if I should feel stupid or not. I think she was going to say something, but a stewardess pushed a cart between us and said, "Would you like something to drink?"

Later, when the stewardess brought our supper, Mom leaned forward and asked us to say grace for ourselves.

I said, "You pray," to Sandy.

"You—you're the oldest," she insisted.

I sighed, ducked my head, and muttered, "Thank you for the food. Amen."

The meal was neat. The main plate was about twice as big as a postcard. There was a bun, butter, jam, a tiny salad, dessert, salt, pepper, and a piece of cheese, each in its own separate container. The silverware was about half the usual size and freezing cold.

I tried to eat very properly, sure that the woman across the aisle was watching me. I snuck a look at her, but she had all her attention focused on the man sitting next to her. They were talking in French and laughing.

By the time we finished eating, the plane was starting its descent to land at Schiphol airport in Amsterdam, Holland. The stewardesses rushed to get all the trays cleared in time for landing.

It was dark, and the plane's lights tipped and swung as we circled the airport. If I leaned forward and Sandy leaned back, I could see the wing in the glow of the flashing red light on its tip. More and more flaps lifted up. The engines quieted, then there was a bump, and the runway lights were tearing past the window.

We were down.

A second later the plane shuddered with the noise of the reverse thrusters. We slowed, stopped, and started taxiing back to the terminal.

"Girls, stay in your seats 'til most of the people are off the plane," Daddy said. "That way we'll miss the rush."

The second the plane stopped, people were on their

feet getting their luggage down. I stood up to get ours out of the overhead compartment.

The woman across the aisle touched my shoulder again and said softly, "I have liked to watch you so much, can you permit me giving you an advice?"

I nodded dumbly.

"I have seen so many—how you call it—adolescents are feeling bad, feeling embarrass by family. You will never make this mistake please. Your family is most nice. To pray is not embarrass. I wish I knew to pray better."

She patted my shoulder, smiled, and followed the man she'd been sitting with down the aisle. I stood there with my mouth open, watching her elegant form until I couldn't see her anymore.

"What did she say?" Sandy asked.

"Nothing," I said and pulled down Sandy's bag.

"Tell me!" she insisted, grabbing her bag.

"It was private," I said and turned my back on her.

"OK, girls, let's go," Daddy said, and I sighed with relief.

We jostled slowly down the aisle, past the stewardesses, who were smiling and shaking everyone's hand. The woman's last phrase kept sticking in my head, "I wish I knew to pray better."

Schiphol airport was so huge and strange that I forgot all about the woman. Sandy didn't even remember to bug me any more about it. All the signs were in about seven languages and had big pictures over them.

We followed Daddy, who seemed to know where he was going, and came to a huge hallway that looked miles long. People were walking along between solid waist-high railings, but they were going as fast as if they were running. Daddy walked straight toward the end of one section and stepped on. It was a moving sidewalk, like an escalator only flat. I grinned and followed.

"You should rest, Kevin," Mom said. "I've heard that there's a lounge here reserved for missionaries. I'd like to find that."

Daddy nodded like he was thinking something over. Then he said, "You're right. I am tired, but we've only got a three-hour layover between flights. I'll rest on one of the couches in the duty-free area so the kids can look around."

"What's he mean, 'duty free'?" Sandy asked me.

I shrugged and said, "It has something to do with taxes. I think we're sort of in between countries, so we don't have to pay any taxes. That makes things cheaper."

Then we were there. The duty-free area was a wide, bright area with very fancy shops. Mom and Daddy sat down on a big, shiny black couch.

"You girls can look around," Daddy said. "Just make sure you're back in an hour."

We nodded and started to take off.

"Don't forget to get something for each of you to give your aunt and uncle," Mom called after us.

Sandy and I walked into the nearest shop. It was full of odd kinds of sausages, cheeses, smoked meat, and fish.

"Hey, Anika," Sandy said, "look at this. Smoked octopus."

I squinched up my nose trying to imagine what that would be like to eat. I kind of liked the octopus we'd eaten at the coast in Kenya, but smoked? Maybe it would turn out to be great, like green eggs and ham in that Dr. Seuss book. For a second I even thought about buying it to see. I giggled and said, "We ought to buy some for Uncle Kurt."

"Gross!" Sandy said. "Mom would probably make us eat it."

"At least we'd find out what it tastes like," I answered. "It costs enough that it ought to be good."

"You're weird," Sandy said.

"Sophisticated people eat all kinds of things," I said, turning my back on her, my nose in the air. Just then I almost collided with the most handsome man I've ever seen. He dodged, a disgusted look on his face, and swept past.

Sandy laughed out loud. I would have kicked her, but she was out of range.

We looked in the other shops and saw raw and cut diamonds, camera and video gear, expensive sports clothes, fancy chocolates, and all kinds of neat things.

"We've only got fifteen minutes left," I said, looking up at a big clock. "We'd better find something for Uncle Kurt and Aunt Doreen."

Sandy made a face, but we started to look. She chose a net bag of tiny round cheeses. I couldn't find anything.

We passed a shop that sold flower bulbs packaged in cardboard boxes. I grabbed the nearest box I could afford and bought it. Then we ran to meet Mom and Daddy.

When we were standing in line to go through security to board our next fight, I took out the box of tulip bulbs and looked at it.

On the bottom was a list of countries with little pictures of flags. Underneath the flags was written, "It is illegal to import these bulbs into countries not on this list."

Canada wasn't on the list. *Oh no,* I thought. *It's against the law to take these tulips into Canada.* I stared at them a second, then stuffed the box into the very bottom of my bag.

The next airplane we were on was almost empty. As soon as the seatbelt sign went off Daddy said, "Let's each find a row of seats and get some sleep. It's already midnight by Kenya time."

I lay on my back across three seats with my knees doubled up so they wouldn't stick into the aisle. Airplane noise filled my head, and the blanket over me was scratchy. I kept worrying about the tulips and thought I'd never go to sleep, but I must have. When I opened my eyes, the window in my row of seats had sunshine in it.

My face felt all squashed and itchy where it had been against the seat. I rubbed it and sat up. Mom saw me and said, "Hi, sleepyhead."

"What time is it?" I asked. My voice was all croaky.

"It's past noon in Toronto, but it's still the middle of the night in Kenya. My watch says 4:30 A.M.," Daddy said, grinning. "You slept a little more than four hours."

I nodded and sat there with my eyes half-open. It looked like morning, but it sure didn't feel like morning. Being out of time with the sun felt very weird. We switched airplanes in Toronto, and by the time we were getting close to Calgary I felt numb all over. I looked over at Daddy and felt even worse. There were huge circles under his eyes, and his skin looked almost gray.

"Anika, go and wash your face and brush your hair so you'll look nice when we land," Mom said.

In the tiny, noisy bathroom, I pulled the brush through my hair, which was sticking out every which way from sleeping. My bangs were sticking up so that the red scar from the cut and all of my forehead showed. I glared at myself. My forehead wasn't really too green and purple anymore. With a sigh, I got the brush wet and tried to make my bangs lie down. Then I jerked at my too-small dress, which was completely wrinkled. I stuck my tongue out at my reflection and went back to my seat.

Sandy was glued to the window. "Look, mountains!"

"Mom said you have to go brush your hair," I said, holding out the brush.

"I did already."

"When, yesterday?" I asked.

She made a face, then grabbed the brush and pushed past me.

I sat in the window seat and looked out. Straight below us the ground looked like a dusty quilt. It was mostly square fields. Some were so dark brown they were almost black, others were kind of gray-brown, and a few were bright green. If you looked way out, there were mountains like a row of broken teeth. I could see the snow on them. The mountains I was used to stood

28

alone, each one by itself: Mount Kenya, Mount Kiliman-
jaro, Longonot. These mountains weren't like that.
They all ran together, making a jagged wall all along
the edge of the land. I stared at them with interest.

Even after the plane landed, I could still see the
mountains along the edge of the world. They made me
feel better. Exciting things could happen in a place with
mountains like that.

In fact, the mountains made me feel so good that I
forgot all about the tulips.

Walking into the airport, I felt like I was made of
wood. My eyes would hardly stay open. We found our
suitcases, then waited in line at customs. Mom kept
anxiously watching the people through the windows.
Just before it was our turn, Mom started waving madly.

"Look, Kevin! There's Kurt."

Daddy smiled and waved, too. I was still trying to figure out who Mom was waving at.

"Is that him?" Sandy asked me. "That tall man?"

I shrugged, but Mom said without looking back,
"Yes. Look, Anika, there's Tianna."

I glanced up and saw a tall man who looked vaguely
familiar. I stared, and he grinned at me and waved. I
sort of half waved back. He was holding on to the shoulder of a kid who was smaller than me. Whew! At least
Tianna didn't look way older than me.

I waved at her, but she just glared at me, then turned her back. Her clothes were even nicer than Lisa's—whose clothes were outstanding—but her hair wasn't even brushed.

Sandy poked me, and I realized we were at the customs desk. The man was holding out his hand for my bag. Without thinking I handed it over and turned back to look at Tianna.

"Could you explain this?" the customs man said curtly.

I whipped around to see him holding the box of tulips.

"Um," I said and stopped.

With a frown, he turned to Daddy and said, "You realize it's illegal to bring these into Canada."

My stomach sank. He thought Daddy had tried to get them in by putting them in my bag where maybe customs wouldn't look as hard.

"I bought them!" I blurted. "They were for my aunt, only I didn't see that we couldn't bring them here 'til we were already on the plane." *Well, almost on the plane,* I thought to myself.

"Anika!" Mom said, frowning. "You should have told us!"

My ears felt hot, but I kept on looking at the customs man. He wasn't looking at me, though. He was frowning at Daddy.

"Take your suitcases and go over to that office, please," he said.

Chapter Three

I swallowed. Those tulips I'd bought were really getting us into trouble. Daddy picked up a suitcase and followed the customs man. You could tell by the way Daddy moved that he was very tired. Mom and Sandy followed him, but I hung back.

"It was only me," I called to the customs man. "Mom and Dad didn't do anything. Daddy's sick; please let us go through."

He didn't even turn around.

"Anika!" Daddy called, and I could tell it was an order. In the other room a fat woman with short blonde hair that stuck out all over went through every tiny part of our luggage, like we were smugglers or something. They even looked in Daddy's medicine bottle and asked about the prescriptions. Sandy kept glaring at me, and Mom and Daddy ignored me.

I wished I was dead.

After a lecture, the fat lady let us go, and we walked out to where Uncle Kurt was waiting. He came over and hugged Mom. I was afraid he'd hug me, too, so I stayed way back. Daddy was beside me because he'd been walking slowly. I'd tried to get him to let me carry the suitcase, but he wouldn't.

Uncle Kurt came over and took the suitcase from Daddy. "Hazel wants us to go straight home so you can rest," he said. "You sure look like you could use it."

Then he looked at me and said, "So *you're* the smuggler in the family. I thought Christians weren't into smuggling." He laughed.

I just stared at my feet. This was terrible.

"Just kidding, just kidding," he said. "Smuggle all you want. Why should you be different from anyone else?" He looked up and raised his voice. "Tianna, come here and meet your smuggling cousin."

She came over and stood about five feet away.

"Tianna, this is Anika. Say hi," Uncle Kurt said, and then he left with Daddy.

Tianna stared at me a second then said "Hi" in a flat voice. Then she added, "Your dress is really gross."

I clenched my fists and answered, "Well, so is your hair."

"I like it this way," she said and walked off.

Everybody was walking now, so I followed. At least Tianna hadn't noticed my forehead. Sandy was holding Mom's hand. I wished I was, too, but I was sure everyone was still mad about the tulips. I glared at Tianna's back. How could God give me such a terrible cousin?

Calgary looked bare. There was almost no one walking and hardly anyone riding bicycles. There were people on bicycles everywhere in Kenya. Here, everybody was in clean, new-looking cars. Even the buses we saw were clean. They weren't anything like the dusty buses at home that were always packed full of people wearing bright clothes.

I'd never seen so many houses packed together, either. They all looked almost the same. We turned off the huge road, then went down more roads with more houses, each on a little piece of grass. The house we finally stopped in front of was bigger than most of the others. I was so sleepy I hardly noticed what the inside of the house looked like on the way to bed.

Loud voices woke me up.

"It's none of your business where I was last night! You are not my keeper, Kurt. Or my boss, either, for that matter!"

It was a woman yelling. Then she started swearing. Suddenly a man's voice broke in.

"Shut up! Shut up! I'm your husband, and I won't have this!" It was Uncle Kurt.

Sandy was sitting up in the other bed. Her eyes were wide and scared. "Is that Aunt Doreen?" she whispered.

I shrugged and then nodded. Uncle Kurt had said he was her husband. It had to be her. She was still yelling.

"Why? Don't you want me to swear while your goody-goody missionary sister is here? You swear well enough yourself most of the time."

"Shut up!" Uncle Kurt bellowed again. "If you can't behave, get out!"

"I will not. This is my house, and you can't tell me what to do. I don't hold with that nonsense that the husband can order his wife around. I'm a person, too, Kurt. Don't let any religious nonsense make you forget that."

There was a slam, and then silence.

"What time is it?" Sandy asked. "Are we supposed to get up?"

We were in a bedroom with two beds. Everything was blue and white and ruffly. It was light outside.

I said, "I don't know. I'm hungry."

We both just stayed still, listening. "It must be morning," I said after a minute. "I smell bacon and coffee."

Breakfast was very weird. Everyone pretended nothing had happened. Aunt Doreen was tall and thin. After hearing her yell, I thought she would look mean, but she just looked kind of sad.

"Tianna, how about you and I take your cousins to the mall today," she said.

"Mommm, it's Saturday." Tianna sounded irritated. "I'm supposed to meet Sharra and Janna this morning."

"For once you can do something with me. You know I don't like you spending time with those kids anyway." I could tell Aunt Doreen was trying hard not to get mad again.

Tianna rolled her eyes and started eating her pancake. Aunt Doreen went out to the kitchen. A second later Tianna went after her. I'd finished eating so I picked up my plate to clear it, but I stopped dead just before I got to the kitchen.

"I won't go to the mall with those geeks, cousins or not!" Tianna was saying. "Did you see the clothes they had on yesterday? And what about what Anika's wearing this morning?"

I backed away from the kitchen and went into the room where Sandy and I had slept. A minute later, Sandy came in. "Come on, you have to go to the mall with Aunt Doreen."

"I'm not going," I answered.

"Mom says you have to," Sandy said.

"How about you? Aunt Doreen said 'cousins'," I demanded.

"I already have permission to stay here. I told Mom I have a sore throat."

"Yeah, right," I said.

"I do!" she insisted and coughed an unconvincing cough. "I said you wanted to go, and Mom said that it's good one of us is going, that it would be a good witness."

"Thanks for nothing," I said.

"Well, I didn't know you didn't want to go when I told Mom," Sandy insisted. "She and Daddy are going to rest. We're not supposed to bother them."

If I argued I'd probably just have to go anyway, and it would make things even more embarrassing. At least Daddy was going to rest. I sighed and stood up. "OK, I'll go."

"Tell me what a mall is like," she said. "I don't remember."

"Come along then," I said.

She shook her head wildly.

"Chicken," I said, and walked out the door wishing I didn't feel so chicken—and wishing I remembered what in the world a mall was like.

On the way to the mall, Aunt Doreen talked the whole time about how nice it was to have visitors from the other side of the world, how good it was for Tianna. I didn't say anything. After what she'd said about Mom when she was yelling at Uncle Kurt, she obviously

36

didn't mean it. Tianna just sat leaning against the car door with her arms crossed, looking out the window. Her hair was brushed, and it had a barrette in it.

Aunt Doreen had just parked the car in a huge parking lot when Tianna said, "Give me two hundred bucks, Mom. I'm going to buy Anika some clothes. If I have to be at the mall with her, at least she can look like a human being."

Aunt Doreen stared at Anika for a second, then said, "What a nice idea. You and Anika can go clothes shopping, and I'll pick you up in a couple of hours."

My mouth fell open. I couldn't believe my ears—or my eyes—as I watched Aunt Doreen just hand Tianna two hundred dollars! She was going to let Tianna buy clothes for me. I shut my mouth and swallowed hard. What would Daddy say? Would we have to pay them back? They probably wouldn't be the kind of clothes Mom would approve of, either.

"Um, I don't think—" I started to say, but Tianna kicked me hard and opened her car door.

"Come on, Anika. Don't just sit there," she said, getting out.

"Have fun, girls. See you later," Aunt Doreen called as she pulled away.

I stood there staring after the car.

"So much for Mom wanting to spend time with me,"

Tianna mumbled. Then she jerked the barrette out of her hair, threw it on the ground, and shook her head so her hair was in her face again.

I bent down to pick up the barrette, but she said, "Leave it!" and marched through the big doors into the mall.

I followed her. I mean, what else could I do?

I looked around. We were in a huge hallway, and there were stores on both sides. Tianna grabbed my arm and hauled me, practically running, down and around a corner and into a store.

"What size are you?" she demanded.

I just stared at her. How was I supposed to know what size I was in Canadian clothes?

She narrowed her eyes and looked me up and down. "You're bigger than me, and I'm a twelve. So you're probably a fourteen." She started jerking things off the rack. "Here, go try these on."

She shoved the clothes at me, but I kept my hands down, my fists clenched. I was very tired of being pushed around.

"Stop it!" I half yelled. "Mom would be really mad if she had to pay your mom back for clothes she didn't even help choose."

"Does your mom still choose your clothes?" Tianna asked. "No wonder you look like such a geek."

"We don't happen to have hundreds of dollars lying around to waste on dumb clothes," I hissed. "My mom and dad are doing more important things than getting rich and spoiled in a boring city."

Tianna gave me a funny look. "You like your parents, don't you?"

"Of course. Don't you like yours?"

She just looked down. She kicked at the side of the bin of sweaters we were standing by, then shrugged. "My parents don't like me, so why should I care about them?" She glared at me like she was daring me to say something.

I couldn't think of anything to say. She laughed at me and said, "Come on, try the clothes on. Your precious mom and daddy won't have to pay for them. Mom gave me the money, and she never cares what I do with it."

The first outfit I tried on was really wild. I laughed at my reflection.

"I guess that's not really you," said Tianna, staring at me critically.

I really liked the clothes I tried on next.

"You're sure Mom and Daddy won't have to pay for this?"

"No way!" Tianna said. "Come on, don't be chicken. I want to go find Sharra and Janna, and we have to get you shoes yet."

"What's wrong with these?" I asked, looking down at my dusty canvas tennies.

Tianna just rolled her eyes.

I was still nervous, but getting new stuff I liked was fun! When I stood up with new leather tennis shoes on, I grinned and said, "Ta-da! Witness the new Anika Scott!"

Tianna laughed, "You're crazy! Come on, let's get your hair fixed."

"Not like yours. Mom would kill me. I don't want to get kicked out completely from my family."

"You and your parents. Do they really care about you?" she asked.

I nodded, "Um-hum, they do."

"Won't the clothes and stuff make them mad?"

"No, they'll just be glad they don't have to buy me so many clothes," I said, crossing my fingers behind my back. I hoped that's what they'd say anyway.

"Come on, let's get your hair done," Tianna said. "Joanne—that's Sharra's sister—works in the mall, and she's really good."

"You should get her to do yours, too," I said. "Is it really in style all messy and in your face like that?"

"No, but at least it isn't nerdy like yours. Besides, it makes Mom mad," she said and took off. I had to practically run to catch up.

It turned out that Joanne wasn't busy, so she said

she'd cut my hair. It didn't feel like it was me at all, sitting in new clothes in a beauty salon. I guess that made it less scary.

I'd never been in a beauty salon before. The place stank of cigarette smoke and permanent chemicals. Joanne was really friendly, though, and kept asking me about Kenya. It made it even stranger to be talking about home. She never said anything about the cut on my forehead. That made me feel good because I figured that must have meant it wasn't very noticeable.

My hair ended up looking like what I thought was sort of Chinese. It was short in back and longer by the line of my jaw.

"This is just perfect for your face," said Joanne, using a brush and a blow dryer at the same time. "Come look at this," she called.

A second later, five or six of the people who worked in the salon were all standing around saying I was gorgeous. Even Tianna was grinning at me. My face felt hot, and I wished I could run out of there—but it was kind of fun, too.

Joanne looked at Tianna and asked, "Your turn now? Do we get to tame your mop head?"

"No way! We've got to go. Come on, Anika." She pulled me toward the door, then stopped and walked back and asked, "How much?"

"It's just five bucks for kids ten and under on Saturdays," Joanne said. "Come on, let me do you, too. We're not busy today, and it's about time you grew up a little."

"Leave my head alone! Here's your five bucks," Tianna said, fishing out the money.

"But I'm twelve!" I insisted.

Tianna kicked me in the ankle. Joanne said, "I didn't hear that," and grinned. "Off with you. Have fun with your cousin, mop head."

"Let's go to McDonald's," Tianna said. "I'm hungry."

"Me too," I said, looking down at my feet in their new tennies. My hair swung against my cheeks. I looked at my reflection in a store window and grinned. I felt like I was in a costume. Anika Scott disguised as a Canadian kid.

I'd probably eaten at a McDonald's when I was seven, but I didn't remember much about it. I stared at the menu up on the wall behind the counter. It didn't make sense. What were Chicken McNuggets, Quarter Pounders, or McDLTs? I felt too stupid to ask. Everybody's food came in paper packets, so even watching didn't help. It smelled good, though.

All of a sudden it was our turn. Tianna rattled off a list of things, then the teenager taking our order looked at me.

"Um . . . ah . . . " I stuttered.

"Well?" Tianna demanded. "What do you want?"

"Um . . ." I could feel the people in line behind us staring at me. "Um . . ." I was thinking frantically. "I'll have the same as her," I blurted, pointing at Tianna. The teenager rattled off the list of things again, and I nodded with relief.

"What was the matter with you?" Tianna asked as we sat down.

I didn't want to answer, so I unwrapped the sandwich Tianna handed me. "It's just a hamburger!" I blurted.

"What did you expect, a lawn mower?" Tianna asked, laughing.

I glared at her. "How was I supposed to know what a McDLT is? It sounds more like a kind of truck."

Tianna nearly killed herself laughing. "You've never been at McDonald's before. So come on, taste your truck," she said between giggles.

I took a bite and then stopped. "What time is your mom coming? She said two hours. Two hours must be up."

"Who cares. She'll find us when she's ready," Tianna said, still giggling. "She never comes when she says anyway."

"I don't want to get in trouble," I insisted. "Maybe she'll come when she said she would because I'm here. Let's go back."

"So eat your truck first," she said, grinning. She giggled again. "You're great. Anika, my smuggling cousin who thinks a Big Mac is a truck!"

I frowned. It wasn't all that funny, especially the part about smuggling. "I wasn't trying to smuggle," I said with my mouth full. "It was just tulip bulbs for your mom. Only they weren't supposed to come into Canada, but I didn't know that." I squirmed and added, "At least, not at first."

Tianna gave me another funny look. "Why would you buy tulip bulbs for my mother?"

I shrugged. I was tired of talking about parents, especially since Tianna acted so weird about it. "Come on, let's go."

Aunt Doreen was there. "Where were you, Tianna!" she demanded. "I've been here for hou—" She stopped mid-sentence and stared at me. "Look at you, Anika! I love your clothes and your hair. Wow! You have great taste."

I squirmed and then remembered my manners. "I'm sorry we're late, Aunt Doreen," I said. "And thank you very much for buying me these clothes and stuff. It was Tianna who helped me choose such nice things."

Maybe now she won't yell at Tianna anymore, I thought. It didn't work.

When I said Tianna's name it was like Aunt Doreen

remembered she was mad. She whirled on Tianna and demanded, "What about it, Tianna? Why were you so late? And if you can help Anika take care of her hair, why can't you do something about your own? Where's the barrette I made you put in this morning?"

Tianna just stared at her and didn't say a word. I wished I could disappear. Nobody said anything else the whole way home.

Chapter
Four

After the miserable ride back from the mall with Aunt Doreen and Tianna mad at each other, I was glad to get out of the car. Going into the house was another matter. What would my parents say about my new clothes and haircut?

Mom and Daddy were talking to Uncle Kurt in the living room. All of them stopped and stared at me.

"Anika, you look terrific," Uncle Kurt said, then everybody was talking at once. I couldn't tell if Mom really liked how I looked or not.

"We will of course pay you back," Daddy said.

"No, you won't," said Aunt Doreen. "Kurt is happy to do anything for his missionary sister and her kids." She gave Uncle Kurt a fierce look and walked out.

"Hey, no fair," Sandy said. "How come you get all these new clothes and I don't?"

"Kurt," Daddy said, "we can't let you do this."

"I didn't do it, my wife did. If for once she does something nice, I'm not going to stop it," Uncle Kurt said.

"Sandy is right, though. We'll have to get her some new clothes, too."

Daddy started to argue, and Mom stood up to leave and motioned me to come with her. She didn't look pleased. Sandy followed us into the bedroom. "Anika, how could you do this?" She was talking really soft so no one would hear us. "You know we don't just take things from people."

I tried to explain how it just kind of happened. "It really wasn't Aunt Doreen anyway. It was Tianna," I ended by saying. "Mom, Aunt Doreen is terrible."

"She's not really terrible," Mom said. "She's just mixed up and very angry. How much money did you spend?"

"Well, Aunt Doreen gave Tianna two hundred dollars. Tianna says nobody cares what she does with money. They must be super rich."

"Yeah," said Sandy. "It won't matter if they buy me clothes then, too."

"Whether they're well off or not has nothing to do with this," Mom said. "I don't feel at all right about taking the money in such a careless way. We can't afford to spend two hundred dollars on one outfit, Anika. We'll just have to take it back."

"Mommm, please?" I begged. "With these clothes I feel almost OK here. I need them. Besides, Uncle Kurt said we should keep them."

"That's enough!" Mom said.

At least they can't take my haircut back, I thought.

It turned out I didn't have to give any of my new stuff back. Daddy said that if we wanted to maintain a good relationship with Uncle Kurt and Aunt Doreen we'd just have to keep the clothes, because Uncle Kurt was absolutely determined that we should.

"I'll get more clothes than you," Sandy said. "I won't waste it all on one outfit."

"So?" I said.

"Come on, let's go watch TV," she said and headed downstairs.

The next day was Sunday, and we didn't go to church. Mom and Daddy both slept until midmorning, then we had a family church like we do when we're camping. Daddy read the Bible and asked us questions. Aunt Doreen didn't get up, but Uncle Kurt and Tianna both sat with us. After church Uncle Kurt stayed and talked to Mom and Daddy for ages.

At lunch he said, "You know, Kevin, I'm starting to think the Bible's worth listening to. I want to get back to a more traditional life-style. You know, women should stay home and serve and obey their husbands."

"Christianity isn't about tradition," Daddy explained. "It's about total submission to a loving God by both men and women. Ephesians chapter five says that the husband should lay down his life for his wife, the way Christ laid down his life for the church."

Uncle Kurt didn't seem to hear. He said, "I think things would be a lot better if people stuck to traditional family roles."

Aunt Doreen walked into the room in her bathrobe just then. She glared at Uncle Kurt's back on her way over to the fridge. I held my breath waiting for the fight, but she grabbed an apple out of the fridge, poured a cup of coffee, and left the room.

After lunch Uncle Kurt said, "OK, who's ready to go to Parkers'?"

It turned out that the Parkers were people he knew who owned a ranch south of Calgary.

"I couldn't let my nieces come to Alberta without getting a look at a real ranch," Uncle Kurt said, poking Sandy in the ribs.

"Do they have horses?" I asked. I'm absolutely crazy about horses. Of course, Sandy asked about kittens because cats are her thing.

Uncle Kurt nodded and laughed. "No respectable ranch would be without horses or kittens."

"Kurt, I'm sorry, but Kevin should take it easy," Mom said as she stacked the dishes. My stomach twisted. Daddy couldn't get tired because then he'd get really sick again.

"I'm sure I could manage, since Kurt has gone to all this trouble," Daddy said. But he looked really tired.

"You promised!" I blurted. "You promised to rest."

"Anika!" Mom said.

"But you did!" I insisted.

"Anika's right, Hazel," Daddy said, "and so are you. I did promise." He turned to Kurt. "There's no reason Hazel and the kids couldn't go. I'm sure Anika and Sandy would just hate that." He looked at us with a twinkle in his eyes.

"You'd better get out of your new clothes, though, Anika," Mom said. "Ranches in the spring aren't the cleanest things in the world. This should be fun."

Tianna had been standing at the door from the hall, watching. Now she said, "I'm going over to Sharra's this afternoon."

"Tianna, get ready," Uncle Kurt snapped at her. "You're coming, too. You haven't been to Parkers' since last fall."

"You never even asked if I wanted to go with you when you went before. What am I supposed to do? Get there by myself or something?" she demanded.

"I don't want any lip from you," he snapped. "I'm offering to take you now, and you're coming whether you want to or not."

When I went to get changed, Tianna followed me

into the bedroom. She sat on my bed, hugged her knees, and said, "I wish my mom and dad were more like yours. It seems like mine are always either yelling at me or fighting with each other."

She looked so sad. "You could come and live with us," I said without thinking. I stuffed my head into a sweatshirt and didn't hear what she said next.

Outside the city we drove for miles down gravel roads that were as straight as a ruler. The land was flat except for the shining white, jagged mountains in the distance. Everything was bare, brown, and muddy. There were humps of dirty snow in the ditches. When we got out of Uncle Kurt's pickup truck, the wind was cold.

"How come everybody here likes spring so much?" I asked, hugging my arms and trying to step around the muddiest patches.

"I guess you have to live through winter to appreciate it," Mom said.

I promised myself right then and there that I'd never live in a place where there was winter.

Mrs. Parker had long, straight hair and a nice smile. She hugged Tianna. "I'm so glad your dad brought you with him. I've missed you," she said. "It's nice to meet your cousins, too."

Mr. Parker shook everybody's hands with a quick jerk

and didn't say anything. He looked like a cowboy, only instead of a cowboy hat he wore a baseball cap that said "Cargill" on it. He wasn't very tall, but he was thin and had on muddy cowboy boots. Mr. and Mrs. Parker had three kids. Sandy took off with two of them to look for kittens.

"Didn't the black-and-white mother have her kittens in the tractor Quonset?" one kid asked as they headed off. "Come on, let's go see if she moved them."

Tianna and I ended up following Dean Parker, who is twelve, to a high wooden fence to look at some muddy horses. The way she was acting, I think Tianna kind of liked Dean.

A big black horse came over toward us. Tianna backed off, and I reached out my hand too quickly. The horse jumped back and crow-hopped twice. The other horses danced away from it, then they all stood and stared at us, their ears all pricked up. They were wonderful.

I don't think Tianna thought so. She backed up even farther when the horses were dancing around. She looked scared.

"Um, I'm going to see the kittens," she said. "You coming, Anika?"

I just shook my head without taking my eyes off of the horses. I'd only been riding twice in Kenya. These horses looked stronger and bigger than the ones there.

"Boy, are you ever lucky," I said to Dean, "having your own horses."

"I don't see what's so great about that," he said. "They're Dad's anyway, and most horses are dumber than a bag of hammers. I'd rather ride an ATV any day. I'm stuck with horses right now because there's too much water in the south quarter to take my three-wheeler through there. Hey, if you think horses are so great, why don't you come with me?"

"With you where?" I asked. "The horses are here." I wasn't about to leave. The black one was coming back over to us again. I put my hand out very slowly. "What kind of horses are they?"

"Quarter horse," Dean said. "JJ here is registered. All of them are, except Babe—that one over there with the white blaze. Dad says she's the best of the lot. Listen, I'm not talking about leaving the horses. I'm talking about taking two of them out to check on the cows in the south quarter."

"Riding?" I asked with a squeak. "You mean going riding?"

He nodded at me like he thought I had no brain.

"Don't we have to ask permission?"

"Look, I have to do this every day. Dad made checking on the south-quarter cow herd my job during the spring calving. It's no big deal."

"That's what *you* think!" I said.

Dean made me stay outside the fence while he caught JJ and Babe and put bridles on them. He led them both out of the gate, then handed me Babe's reins. He sort of vaulted onto JJ's back and said, "Come on."

I swallowed nervously. Bareback riding! Well, I wasn't going to chicken out now. I put the reins over Babe's head, then I tried to climb on. It didn't work. Babe looked back at me. I tried again.

"Haven't you ever been riding before?" Dean asked, laughing. He got down and took Babe over to the wooden fence. "Climb on from there."

Babe's back seemed very high up—not to mention slippery—as we followed JJ down the driveway. I copied how Dean was holding the reins. It was different than how I'd learned in Kenya. *Western riding,* I thought and grinned.

We rode down the side of the road a little way, then through a gate into wide-open, taffy-colored grassland.

"Heeya!" Dean yelled, and he and JJ took off at a dead run. Big globs of mud flew up from JJ's hooves. With a lunge, Babe tore after them. I let go of the reins and grabbed her mane, holding on with my knees and hands like I'd never let go. I could feel Babe's huge muscles moving underneath me and the wind blowing in my face. I was both petrified and wildly happy all at the same time. Babe tore through an enormous puddle, and water sprayed up from her hooves in all directions.

We tore past Dean, and he yelled, "Pull back on the reins, stupid!"

I let go of Babe's mane with one hand and made a grab for the reins, which luckily were tied together so they hadn't dropped. I pulled back hard, and Babe practically sat down. I went over her head in a somersault and landed in another puddle. Babe just stood there looking at me.

"Are you all right?" Dean yelled as he galloped over.

I nodded, and he started laughing. "That was some dismount. You're lucky Babe ground ties or you'd have to catch her again. I'm going to check the cows, then I'll be right back."

He trotted off. I stood up and reached for Babe's reins. She snorted softly and rubbed her head up and down my front. I laughed rather shakily. My muddy, wet pants stuck to my legs, and I shivered. Dean was nowhere in sight. I hugged Babe's neck and wondered if I could get up on her back again. At least my seat would be warmer there.

There was a big rock about a hundred yards away. I led Babe over. She stood still, and I managed to scramble on all by myself. "You're the best horse ever," I said, rubbing her neck. "You couldn't help it if I told you to stop too fast."

I was rubbing her neck and trying not to shiver when Dean came tearing back over a rise.

"There's a cow calving, and I can see four hooves. She needs help. I've got to stay with her so she doesn't wander off," he called. "Go get Dad, OK?" He took off without waiting for an answer.

I managed to get Babe to turn around and start back. She didn't act like she understood the way I was using the reins. I kicked with my heels and she started to trot. My sore seat bounced all over her back. *Running is better than this,* I thought as I just about bounced off and clutched crazily at her mane. I kicked harder and yelled like Dean had, and Babe started galloping. This time I hung on to the reins. Babe seemed to know where to go.

Luckily Dean had left the gate open. Babe's head went down and she ran faster. Gravel flew in all directions as we tore down the driveway. I saw a bunch of people standing outside the house. I pulled back slowly on the reins, and Babe actually started to slow down.

Mr. Parker took two big steps and stood in the driveway with his hands up. "Whoa, girl. Easy, girl," he said, loud but kind of gentle. Babe stopped right in front of him.

"Dean says for you to come to help a cow with four hooves," I said, breathing hard.

"What?" he asked.

"Well, that's what he said! Four hooves showing," I answered.

Both Mr. and Mrs. Parker laughed. "That means he could see four hooves of a calf showing, sticking out a little way, on a cow who is calving," explained Mrs. Parker. "Either she's having twins or one calf is all twisted up. Either way, she'll need help."

Mr. Parker was already on his way across the yard at a trot. I wasn't sure how to get off of Babe. I'd never gotten off of a horse without stirrups before—except in the pasture, and that hadn't been exactly normal. I put both legs on one side and sort of slid off. My feet hit the ground with a thud and I nearly fell down.

Mom caught me. "Anika, what on earth?" she said. "You're soaked and freezing. How do you get yourself into these crazy situations?"

Already Mr. Parker was back with a saddle. He put it on Babe, cinched it up, and swung onto Babe's back in no time. He hung a coiled rope over the saddle horn and reached down for a bag of stuff his wife handed him. He and Babe left at an easy lope.

As soon as he was gone, Mom and Mrs. Parker hustled me into the house to get cleaned up. I was so muddy I had to have a bath while Mrs. Parker put my clothes in the wash. I didn't care. I'd ridden a quarter horse bareback and had actually done something helpful. I couldn't stop grinning. By the time I got out of the tub, supper was on the table.

Tianna glared at me as I came into the kitchen. "You think you're so cool, going riding with Dean Parker," she hissed. She turned her back on me and went and sat down.

I sighed. Couldn't she figure out that I only cared about the horses?

Dean and Mr. Parker came in a bit late and had to go wash up. I had to tell my part of the story all over again for Mr. Parker. When I got done, he said, "I always did say that Babe had a lot of sense. Not that I can say the same for my son, putting a green rider up bareback."

"Is the cow OK?" I asked.

"Yeah, nice twin heifer calves. Dean and I did all right with that cow, so maybe we'll keep Dean after all," Mr. Parker said with a grin.

Halfway through supper Tianna and Sandy went out to look at the kittens one last time without asking me if I'd come. I was too warm and sleepy anyway. Besides, my seat was hurting where I'd fallen off of Babe. When we went out to the truck, Tianna and Sandy were already sitting in the back.

On the way home they were quiet and kind of giggly. My eyes kept wanting to shut, but my sore behind— and Uncle Kurt's loud country and western music— kept me from going all the way to sleep. I didn't pay any attention to how weird Sandy and Tianna were acting. Until I heard a soft mew, that is.

My eyes flew open.

Tianna's jacket was mewing! I sat up and stared at her. Both she and Sandy made frantic hushing noises at me.

The jacket mewed again.

Chapter
Five

〜〜〜〜〜〜

Luckily, Uncle Kurt's music was too loud for him and Mom to hear anything. I sure wasn't going to tell. If there's one thing you learn at boarding school, it's to not be a tattletale.

"Can I see it?" I whispered.

Tianna shook her head no.

"Come on, I don't care about Dean. I just wanted to go riding. Please?" I begged.

Tianna opened her jacket, and a little tabby kitten with blue eyes and white on its little nose and chin looked up at me. Its pink mouth opened in a loud, scared mew.

Tianna covered the kitten up in a hurry, but Mom looked back at us.

"Mew!" Sandy said. "Mew, mew!"

It was a pretty good imitation.

"What on earth?" Mom asked.

"She's pretending to be a kitten," I explained.

Mom gave Sandy a puzzled look, but turned back around.

"Thanks!" Tianna whispered. "You guys are brilliant."

We were just pulling into Tianna's driveway, and Daddy was coming to the door to meet us. I opened the door to get out—and groaned. I couldn't believe how stiff I was!

Sandy got out and kind of blocked Daddy's view of Tianna as she rushed past him, her jacket in her arms. Sandy went after her, but I couldn't get away without telling Daddy about riding. I didn't mind, really.

"Tianna!" Aunt Doreen almost screamed. She was standing in the door to Tianna's room. "Kurt! Kurt, come here!" Boy, did she ever sound mad. "Look what your daughter's brought back from that ranch! A *cat!* I will not have a cat in my house."

"Your house?" Uncle Kurt roared. "I'll have you know I'm the master of this house. Right, Kevin? The husband is the master."

"Kur—" Daddy started to say, shaking his head warningly.

Uncle Kurt didn't listen. He just broke in angrily, yelling at Aunt Doreen. "If my daughter wants to have a kitten, it's up to me to say if she can or not. I say it might do some good to have something gentle and pretty in this house. We sure don't get much gentleness from you."

"Your hyperreligious sister and her husband are making you even worse, if that's possible," snapped Aunt Doreen. "I don't think you realize that women are people. We're individual human beings who have every right you have, Kurt Malcome! If this isn't my house, then where do I live?" Now her face was all red, and I could tell she was trying not to cry. She whirled to go.

"My daughter can have a kitten if I say so, woman," he bellowed at her retreating back. She just kept going.

There was a long silence.

Uncle Kurt shuffled his feet, like a little kid who is embarrassed. "Um, sorry about that, folks," he said. "I just don't get the kind of respect around here that a man deserves in his own house."

"Kurt," Daddy said softly. "It's true that a man is to be head of his household, but the Bible teaches that a leader is to act and live for the benefit of those in his care. He's to give respect to others as well."

Uncle Kurt gave Daddy a puzzled look. I didn't stay to hear more. When I opened the door to Tianna's room, she and Sandy were huddled over the kitten staring at the door wide-eyed.

Tianna looked like she might cry.

"He said you could keep the kitten," I reminded her.

She just barely nodded.

"What are you going to call him?" I asked.

Tianna didn't answer.

"Jake," Sandy said. "We decided at the Parkers'." She had the kitten in her lap.

"Here," I said. Reluctantly Sandy handed it to me. Its little body felt warm in my hands.

"How do you know it's a boy?" I asked.

"The kids said so," Sandy answered.

Jake struggled and mewed really loud. I put him down, and he scratched at the rug and then squatted.

"Oh no!" said Tianna. "He peed on the floor!" She rushed to get a Kleenex. "Mom will kill him," she said, crouching to wipe up the wet spot. The kitten leaned against her foot, yawned, tried to lick a white paw, and lay down with a flop.

"He's so cute," Tianna said in a completely different tone of voice, stroking the little round striped head with one finger. "I just have to keep him."

"Then you better get cat litter and stuff," Sandy said, reaching down to pat Jake, who shut his eyes with a tiny sigh.

Tianna carefully scooped Jake up with both hands, laid him on her bed, and said, "I guess I'll have to ask Dad."

She left the door open, and a second later Uncle Kurt's voice sounded, loud and angry. I went to see what was happening.

"I said you could have a cat," Uncle Kurt snapped,

still sounding angry, "but I won't pay for it. *You* wanted a cat, *you* pay for the junk it needs."

"I can pay, Dad, I can really," Tianna pleaded, "but the only place open now is Super Store. I can't walk there."

"So take the bus," he said and crossed his arms.

Aunt Doreen came storming back into the room, and I backed into the kitchen. "You really are a jerk, Kurt," she yelled, and then she swore at him. "Get in the car, Tianna. I'll take you."

"What's so bad about wanting Tianna to learn some responsibility?" Uncle Kurt yelled. "Why do you always cross me?"

Aunt Doreen wouldn't even look at him as she walked out the door after Tianna.

Uncle Kurt glared at Mom and Daddy and came striding into the kitchen. I pressed myself back against the wall, but he went straight out the door without even looking at me.

"I don't think he heard a word you said," Mom said to Daddy sadly.

The next morning Tianna came into our room, carrying Jake, who was squirming and mewing. "You aren't coming to school here, are you?" she asked.

"Why?" I demanded. "Don't you want us to?"

She shrugged and said, "I guess," in a flat voice. It was obvious that she didn't. I frowned.

"Mom!" Sandy yelled.

When Mom answered from the kitchen, Sandy yelled, "Do we have to go to school?"

Mom walked into the room and said, "Daddy and I decided we wouldn't send you until we get the results from his medical tests. There's no reason for you to have to adjust to a new school only to find out that we're going back right away. You'll both have to work to keep up with your class in Kenya, though. Tianna, don't hold the kitten so tightly. You'll hurt—"

"All right! No school!" Sandy yelled, interrupting.

"Ow!" Tianna said and dropped Jake. "He scratched me!"

Sandy rushed to pick up the kitten.

"Sandy," Mom said, "let him walk. Animals aren't toys. Jake is God's creature, too. Has anybody fed him this morning?"

"You can feed him," Tianna said to Sandy. "I've got to go."

I was still mad about Tianna not wanting me in her class. I plopped onto the bed, frowning furiously. I didn't want to go to school, but I didn't want her to think I was a geek, either.

Sandy and I stayed in the house by ourselves that day

because Daddy and Mom went to the hospital for some of Daddy's tests. I spent most of the day staring at the TV and was feeling crabby when Mom and Daddy came home in the middle of the afternoon.

"Did they come out all right?" Sandy asked as soon as they got into the house. "Did your tests come out all right?"

"They don't know right away, silly," I said.

"Anika's right," Daddy said. "We'll just have to wait."

He sat in a chair in the living room, and Mom made me help her get supper. Sandy was tearing up and down the hall dragging a string for Jake and screaming and giggling when he chased it.

How come I always have to work? I thought. Next time Sandy tore into the kitchen, I yelled, "Hush! You'll bother Daddy!"

Sandy stopped and looked worried, but Daddy had heard. "No," he said, "I'm fine. Anika, will you come here a minute?"

I looked at Mom, and she nodded. "I can finish this. Thanks for helping, Anika. I appreciate it." She smiled at me and I felt a little better.

Daddy was holding a book when I walked into the living room. "I want you to do a social studies report on the Rocky Mountains for me," he said. "This is a great book."

I groaned. Even in Canada, I couldn't get away from schoolwork.

I really missed Kenya that week. There was nowhere to go outside, just streets and houses. I spent a lot of time reading the book Dad had found on the Rocky Mountains. It was about trout fishing, rock climbing, hunting on horseback, skiing, glaciers, and grizzly bears. I could see the mountains out the living room window, and I would stare at them and wish I was somewhere else. Kenya would be best, but those mountains stirred me up inside, too. I wondered if I'd ever see them close-up.

That night at supper, Mom glanced at Tianna. "Tianna, we missed you after school," she said. "Did you have to stay for a project?"

Tianna gave Mom a scared look, then ducked her head.

"Tianna, were you at the mall again?" Uncle Kurt demanded. "I've told you a hundred times I want you home, in this house, immediately after school!"

"Kurt, don't be such a lout," Aunt Doreen said, sounding angry.

"You stay out of this," he yelled. "This week is the first week we've had home-cooked meals and eaten together as a family for years, and that's no thanks to you."

"So why is it my responsibility?" Aunt Doreen demanded. "You can cook as well as I can, Kurt Malcome. I'm not your maid, and Tianna isn't your slave." She slammed down her fork and got up to leave. Then, just at the door, she whirled and said, "You stand up for yourself, Tianna."

"You *will* stop going to the mall, Tianna," Uncle Kurt thundered. "I don't like those kids you hang out with one little bit. I don't want any more reports of you swearing and fighting at school, or of you skipping school, either. Do you hear me?"

Tianna's head was down, but she nodded.

Uncle Kurt grunted and kept eating.

"I don't see what he's so uptight about," Tianna said in our room later. "He never usually even asks what I do. The only way he finds out I've skipped school is when the school calls him. I go to the mall most days after school and get home just before he and Mom do. Why should I come home when no one else is here? What am I supposed to do? Sit and watch TV by myself? As if he cared. Man, I wish I could go to boarding school like you guys do. No parents to hassle you."

"I like home better," I said. Then I paused and sighed. "We might have to stay here, you know, if Daddy's tests don't turn out right."

Tianna frowned and said, "You wouldn't like my school. It's the pits. Tell me about Africa."

I told her about the Mumbu tree, the ibises calling in the morning, the way giraffes looked against the sky when the sun was going down, how Mt. Longonot looked purple when storms came up the Great Rift Valley, and the sounds of lions in the night.

I missed it so much.

"You said I could come live with you if I wanted, right?" she asked. I nodded. I wasn't really sure if she could, but I'd said so and I couldn't back out now.

She didn't really say any more about it, though. I was glad.

Friday night at supper Uncle Kurt said, "You can't come to Calgary without going to the mountains."

I held my breath and thought, *The Rocky Mountains! Oh boy!*

"What do you say to a skiing trip tomorrow, up at Sunshine Village?" he asked.

"Isn't skiing with snow?" asked Sandy, puzzled. "There's no snow here."

Even Aunt Doreen laughed at that.

"Maybe not here, honey," Uncle Kurt said, "but spring skiing is great in the mountains."

At ten o'clock Saturday morning I was at the top of

Strawberry run, the beginners' run, at Sunshine Village. There was deep snow everywhere, making it look like the world was covered with a shining white glaze. The ground dropped away in a smooth, wide trough, and people in bright clothes zipped and swayed down past me.

Standing there in borrowed clothes and rented skis, I felt like I was on another planet. I was trying to stand still. I hung on to my ski poles like grim death because my skis kept wanting to go downhill without my permission.

"Come on, Anika," Tianna called. "Just do like I do."

She shoved off with her poles, zipped on a diagonal across the run, turned, stopped, and looked back.

"That looks easy!" I yelled and shoved off. I whooshed down and across and up, straight at Tianna, then I slipped backwards and fell into the snow. It was fun!

Laughing, she hauled me out. "You've got to dig the edges in to turn," she explained. "Just kind of lean the way you want to go, like you do when you're on a bike."

I'd just finished getting straightened out and back on my skis when Sandy went by, right down the middle of the run. She skied on one ski, then the other, waved her poles wildly in the air, and once nearly turned in a circle before she finally fell down. Uncle Kurt helped her up.

"Stupid skis!" I heard her yell.

Tianna was giggling so hard she nearly choked. My next try wasn't much better. My skis crossed, and when I jerked them apart they headed off in different directions. I hit the snow with a thump. Cold snow sprayed into my face and down my neck. I ended up lying on my face, with my skis crossed behind my back.

Tianna had let me go first. She skied over to me and stopped with the snow flying up from her skis.

"It's not fair," I said, spitting out snow.

"What?" she asked.

"You do that so easily," I said as I tried to get a ski out from behind my back. All I managed to do was stick the end of it into the snow so that it stood up on end. I jerked it out and rolled onto my back. That was better, until I started to slide downhill.

Tianna tried to grab me, but she fell down, too. We lay there giggling. When I finally got straightened out and tried to stand up on one ski, it slid away. I fell again, giggling.

"Dig your edges in so you can stand still, silly," Tianna said.

I did and it worked. "How come your mom came with us?" I asked.

"She's a really good skier," Tianna said and made a face. "I guess she wanted to come skiing bad enough to put up with Dad and me."

She shoved off without looking back. I stood and watched her ski gracefully down to the bottom of the run and out of sight. I looked around again. Some people weren't on skis. They had brightly colored boards, kind of like skateboards. I watched one kid twist and turn like he was surfing. That looked fun. I grinned and shoved after him. That time I actually did two turns before I fell.

I didn't see Tianna again that morning, but I was too busy figuring out how to ski to mind. At first Uncle Kurt and Sandy were around, but then I didn't see them anymore, either. That was OK, though—skiing was getting to be more fun every time I made it down Strawberry run. The lift was just about the best part—after I figured out how to get on and off, that is. I loved the feeling of riding up in the air over the white snow, dark trees, and bright skiers. It was all wide-open space with mountains and snow shining in the sun. The sky was dark blue, and even the air tasted good.

"What's that mountain called?" I asked, pointing at a high peak that gleamed white against the sky.

"That's Brewster," said the lady next to me on the lift. "You can ski down right from the top."

"How do you get up there?" I asked.

She turned and pointed way down at a line of skiers

waiting for a lift. Then we got dumped off at the top of Strawberry again.

I only fell once on the way down that time. I went further down the hill so I could be in the line to go up Brewster Mountain. I wasn't going to be that close to a mountain without going to the top.

At the top I followed the other skiers away from the lift to a wide, flat space. I stood and looked around. It was windy and bare. The back side of the mountain must have been a cliff because there was a sign that said, "No skiers beyond this point." The flat space stopped just beyond the sign—all you could see were the bottom of a valley and mountains rising up on the other side. That was miles and miles down, away from us.

A skier went past me, and I watched him go down . . . and gulped. The run looked like it went almost straight down. Another skier went past and into a whole steep field of big round snow bumps. His legs were working like pistons as he flew from one bump to the next.

How did I ever get myself into this? I thought and shivered. Bunches of people zipped past me. I looked around for an easier way down. There were posts with signs on them. One had a blue square and another had a black diamond. Further away I could see one with a green dot. I wondered what they meant. None of them seemed to point to an easy way down, not that I could see, anyway.

I looked around for help. Everyone zipped past without even looking at me.

I really had done something stupid this time.

Chapter Six

I shivered again, harder. Obviously I couldn't stay where I was. I had to get down off the top of Brewster Mountain.

"Please God, help me get down from here in one piece," I prayed. "I don't want to get hurt."

I swallowed and looked down at all the skiers bouncing and dodging down the mountain in their brightly colored outfits.

"Here goes nothing!" I said and headed at an angle down over the humps of snow.

Bump, bump. Whoosh!

A kid on a snow board almost hit me. He swore and yelled, "Get off the hill if you can't ski, ditz brain!"

"That's what I'm trying to do!" I yelled back, but he was miles away by then. I tried to turn and ended up going almost straight down. After the first two bumps I was in the air. Wow! I hit the ground with my skis under me and was in the air again. I landed hard and there were skis, poles, hard bumps of snow, and blue sky all over. When I finally came to a stop, I lay still for a minute, breathing hard. Then I shook myself and sat up.

Well, at least I was further down—and I was getting good at getting untangled and on my skis again.

I headed down slowly again. Before long, I'd lost track of how many times I'd fallen. Once my leg had gotten wrenched hard, and my left shoulder hurt, too. Skiers kept dodging past me, and twice I'd almost been hit. After another fall, I dug myself out of the snow and climbed onto my skis again, trying not to cry. I swallowed and shook my head. It wouldn't do any good to cry now. I had to get down. "Please help, God," I whispered.

There were two signs in front of where I was standing. One had a blue square on it. The other had a black diamond.

I decided that the part I could see of the run by the black diamond looked easier. I'd just started for it when someone said, "Anika! It *is* you. What on earth are you doing here?"

It was Aunt Doreen. I groaned. *I asked for help, God, but I didn't want her,* I thought desperately.

"Um . . . ," I stammered, feeling stupid. "Um. I wanted to see the top of the mountain."

"But you're heading for a black diamond run," she said. "And you missed lunch."

I suddenly realized I was terribly hungry. My shoulder and leg ached, and I was so tired. . . . Suddenly, the tears I'd been holding back started to spill out, and I couldn't stop them.

"Hey, it's not that bad," Aunt Doreen said and put her arm around me.

I cringed away from her and started forward. She grabbed the back of my jacket, and I fell.

"Leave me alone!" I yelled.

"But Anika, you can't go that way. It's a black diamond run, an expert run." She sounded almost desperate.

I looked at the top. "It looks easier than the other one to me!" I said angrily. "Besides, why should you help me? You don't want us goody-goody missionaries visiting you anyway!"

There was a dead silence. Then Aunt Doreen's face twisted ruefully. "I never could control my tongue," she said. Then she sighed. "Want you or not, I certainly don't want to have to take you to the hospital. That run is one of the most difficult runs at Sunshine. Come on, rest for a few minutes until you feel better, and I'll help you get down the intermediate run."

I looked at her for a second, then nodded.

I was pretty scared when we finally started down, but before long I realized that God really had sent me good help. Aunt Doreen planned one step at a time, and she seemed to know every single bump on the run.

"OK, see that big mogul over there," she said, pointing. It turned out that the humps of snow were called moguls. "You ski across and stop just uphill of it. I'll be right behind you." I did, and she did, and then she pointed out the next place for me to go.

A few stops later, she smiled at me. "You'd be a good skier if you stuck around here. I wish Tianna had half the jam you do."

I looked at her, uncertain. "Half the what?" I asked. She smiled again.

"Half the jam—you know, guts, courage. You don't seem to be afraid of trying anything." Then a frown crossed her face. "Too bad I can't say the same thing for Tianna." I shifted my weight from one foot to the other, feeling uneasy. Why was she always down on Tianna?

"Head just downhill of that tree," she said. "Stop when you get to the other side of the run."

I pushed off. One edge of my skis stuck in the snow and I fell. Furiously I straightened my skis out and tried to stand. The uphill ski slipped and I was down again.

"Take it easy," Aunt Doreen said, catching my arm. "Just go slow and it's not so hard."

I looked up at her, puzzled, then blurted, "You can be really nice."

She laughed and said, "Don't sound so surprised."

"But you're always mad at Tianna and fighting with Uncle Kurt," I said, then gasped and put my hand over my mouth.

"Things don't always turn out the way you want," she said. Then she looked at me sharply. "Let me give you a piece of advice. Don't let that religion of yours pull the wool over your eyes. Don't ever marry a man who thinks women are less than human. Men in your religion tend to do that."

The way she said that made me mad. "You don't know anything about it!" I almost yelled. "Daddy does not think women are less than human, and neither does God!"

"So why did Jesus pick only men disciples, then?" she asked. But before I could answer, she gave an impatient sigh. "Sorry. I'm letting my mouth get away from me again. Come on, let's get off of this hill."

I was quiet the rest of the way down. Aunt Doreen's question bugged me. Why *didn't* Jesus pick any women disciples? I decided to ask Daddy as soon as I could. Until then, I'd just shove the question out of my head.

It felt really good to reach the bottom of the run. And I'd never tasted anything half as good as the hamburger Aunt Doreen bought me back at the lodge. She had a cup of coffee and sat with me while I ate. I watched her, munching slowly so I could enjoy every bit of my burger. She was kind of nice. *If only she'd be nice to Tianna,* I thought.

"You know, Tianna was sad and mad when you didn't come shopping with us." I said. "Don't you like her?"

She gave me a hard look, and I held my breath. I'd really put my foot in it this time. I could almost see her thinking, *Who do you think you are?*

Then she laughed.

"You really do have a lot of jam. I'll bet you have as much trouble with your mouth as I do," she said.

I squirmed, but said, "Well?"

Aunt Doreen shrugged and sighed, "I love Tianna, but it seems like she sets out to antagonize me. She's always either fighting with me, or running away from me, or trying to avoid me. She's been having trouble at school, too, skipping school and fighting. She won't talk to me. She'd probably be better off without me." She was looking down into her coffee cup, and she looked very sad. She shook her head and looked up. "Enough of true confessions for one day. I'm going ski-ing. You coming?"

I grinned and nodded. I was tired and sore, but I wasn't about to quit.

Uncle Kurt was at the lift. I was a ways behind Aunt Doreen, so he didn't see me.

"Where have you been all day, Doreen?" he demanded. "Off having fun while I'm stuck with the kids?" He glared at her.

"If that's what you think, I'm sure you're correct," she snapped back. "After all, you're the boss." She went straight past him.

I took a deep breath, touched his jacket, and tried to explain how Aunt Doreen had helped me. He just grunted, still glaring after Aunt Doreen over my head.

Two days later, I was still sore and tired.

"Good news!" Daddy said as soon as he and Mom walked in after lunch. "My liver is fine."

Sandy and I both came running. "We can go home then, right?" Sandy asked.

Sandy was clutching Jake with both arms. He mewed loudly in protest. Sandy said, "Oh, sorry, Jake," and put the kitten down. She and Jake were together all the time.

"Well?" I demanded.

"The doctors want to do more tests," Mom said, "but yes, we probably cab go hobe."

It was like joy started at my belly button and zoomed up through the top of my head. Sandy and I both yelled and danced around.

"We cab go hobe! We cab go hobe!" I said, laughing at how Mom had muddled the words. Sandy joined in, and we danced around the room yelling, "We cab go hobe!"

Mom and Daddy were laughing, too. Then Sandy ran to Daddy and hugged him, and we ended up with everybody in a great big family hug.

I leaned back, looked up at Daddy's face, and asked, "But why have you been so tired if you're not sick?"

He laughed. "Apparently it's just a persistent infection. The doctor said that a course of antibiotics should clear it up, and then I'll be good as new."

"Let's pack!" I said, heading for our room.

"Not so fast," Daddy said. "The doctors want me to stay until they're sure the infection is cleared up. Besides, we want to visit some of our churches."

Tianna came home right after school that day.

"We get to go back to Kenya," I said, following her into her room.

"You're lucky," she said. "I wish I could leave. Today was the pits. I got sent to the principal for swearing at Mr. Pack, but the jerk deserved it. Sharra won't talk to me, and I don't know why." She flopped onto her bed with her hair straggling into her face.

Sandy had followed us in. Jake jumped off her shoulder and onto the bed. Tianna shoved the kitten away from her, and he fell off the bed.

"Hey!" Sandy objected.

Tianna kicked at Jake in a halfhearted way. "Go on!" she said. "Even you don't like me. Mom hates me, Dad hates me, my friends hate me. You were supposed to be my cat, and even you hate me."

The kitten jumped back with his front feet in the air and pounced on her shoe.

"He does not hate you!" Sandy insisted.

Tianna just made a face at her and said, "Be real! You've completely stolen Jake from me." She reached down and grabbed him by the neck. "Here, get him out of here," she said, shoving the mewing kitten at Sandy.

Sandy grabbed him and left. Tianna just sat there staring at the floor.

I shifted uneasily and said, "When we go, Jake will like you best. Especially if you feed him and stuff."

"You sound like Dad—'Don't forget to feed the cat.'"

I bit my lip. "I don't think your mom and dad really hate you," I said. "Anyway, your mom told me she loves you."

"She sure has a weird way of showing it," Tianna said, shuffling her feet on the rug.

"Maybe if you didn't keep trying to bug her so much?" I said.

Tianna flipped over onto her stomach and started bawling. She half yelled through her sobs, "I can't help it! I can't! She hates me anyway. Everybody hates me. I wish I could just stop being alive."

She buried her face in her pillow and kept sobbing really loud. I stared at her with my mouth open. What could I say? I thought about just sneaking out of the room.

"Please help, God," I whispered. Then it hit me. *Of course! You love her!*

OK, Anika, tell her, I thought. She was crying a little bit quieter now. I swallowed and said, "God loves you." It was kind of hard to get the words out, but I kept talking. "At boarding school, I was all by myself—you know, kind of sad and scared. I used to sing 'Jesus Loves Me'. I know that's a little kids' song, but it really helped."

Tianna looked up at me from under her shaggy bangs. Her nose was running.

I swallowed and kept on. "Jesus really does care, you know. He sent your mom to keep me safe when we were skiing. She showed up just before I almost accidentally went down a black diamond run. God made Daddy's medical tests turn out right, too."

She looked down and didn't answer. In spite of everything that I was saying, I couldn't stop myself from thinking that Jesus sure hadn't answered our prayers about Tianna's family. Things just kept getting worse.

"He does love you," I insisted.

She sniffed loudly. "Maybe if I could get out of here things would be OK. Maybe if I was at your house?"

"I don't know," I said.

"I can come if I want, right?" she asked, looking hopeful.

I couldn't tell her I didn't really know, not now, so I just nodded. I knew I'd better hurry up and talk to Mom and Daddy about it.

That night it was just our family and Tianna. Uncle Kurt was away on a business trip. We waited for ages, but Aunt Doreen didn't come home. Finally we sat down to eat the stew and chapaties Mom had made. It was the best meal yet because nobody yelled at anyone else. Nobody even acted tense or nervous until Sandy wrecked it.

"How come your mom didn't come home?" she asked Tianna.

Tianna just shrugged. I tried to kick Sandy, but couldn't reach her. She wouldn't quit. "How come she never cooks supper or anything? My mom always cooks supper for our visitors—"

Mom and Daddy both interrupted at once.

"Sandy, that's enough!" Daddy said.

"Don't be so quick to judge, Sandy!" Mom said. She looked at Daddy, then went on. "We can't see into Aunt Doreen's life, so we can't really know why she does things the way she does. Anyway, you're wrong about me cooking. Atanas usually cooks for both us and our guests."

"Not on Sunday!" Sandy blurted, and everybody laughed.

"You would never just not come home, or let your guests cook the whole time like Aunt Doreen," Sandy insisted.

"That's enough!" Daddy said again. "Now drop it, or I'll send you from the table."

Just then the phone rang, and Tianna ran to get it. I think she was glad to get away from the table.

"Uncle Kevin," she called, "it's for you, and it sounds like it's long distance."

Daddy went to the phone, then returned to the table a few minutes later. "Well, that was Paul Stewart calling from Kenya. He said we're needed back in Kenya urgently. One of the other Bible school teachers had to leave unexpectedly, and term starts in two weeks."

"What about the other tests?" Mom asked.

"I'm booked for tomorrow morning," Daddy said. "I'll get some done then and ask if the rest are necessary or could be done in Kenya."

"We're going back right away!" I yelled and jumped up from the table.

Sandy was up, too. She started yelling, "We cab go hobe! We cab go hobe!" and dancing around the table.

"Not before you finish your supper," Daddy said with a grin. "Sit down."

Tianna stayed sitting at the table with her head down. She slowly shoved the food around her plate.

The next couple of days were crazy. We spent hours shopping with Mom for stuff we couldn't get in Kenya, and for stuff other people had asked us to bring back. Sandy never did get the money from Uncle Kurt for clothes. I guess he forgot, and Mom and Daddy said we weren't allowed to ask.

Tianna acted kind of weird. Half of the time she acted like I was her best friend, and then she wouldn't even talk to me.

She acted weird with the kitten, Jake, too. Sometimes she carried him all over the house and wouldn't put him down, and other times she completely ignored him. Mostly she forgot to feed him. Sandy didn't mind, though. That way Jake was more like her own kitten.

In fact, now that we were leaving, Sandy begged and begged to take the kitten with us. "Tianna doesn't like Jake, and nobody feeds him but me," she pleaded.

"Sandy, he isn't your cat," Mom said.

"He is!" Sandy insisted. "He'll starve here."

"Tianna won't let Jake starve, and neither will her parents," Daddy said.

"They will," Sandy insisted, crying.

"We can't take a kitten back with us, and that's final," Daddy said.

The day before we left Tianna didn't come home until after supper, and she reeked with the smell of cigarette smoke.

"That's it!" bellowed Uncle Kurt. "Get to your room. You deserve a whipping, and this time you're going to get it."

"Don't you dare whip that child," said Aunt Doreen as soon as Tianna slammed her door.

"*You* won't discipline her. She's going to end up just like you, completely self-centered, with no discipline or sense of responsibility. I intend to pound some sense into her."

"If you so much as leave a welt on that child, I'll report you for child abuse!" Aunt Doreen yelled as Uncle Kurt stamped out of the room after Tianna.

He whirled at her words. "Child abuse! Right!" he bellowed. "I'd like to report you for family destruction, but the stupid law doesn't recognize the kind of damage you cause!" He kept arguing and seemed to forget about Tianna.

I went into Tianna's room. She was sitting on her bed, her head down.

"I wish I was going with you tomorrow," she said. I couldn't tell if her voice was full of tears or anger.

"Why don't you ask?" I said. I still hadn't talked to Mom and Daddy about it. To be honest, I was scared to, but there was no way they could say no, was there? Then I remembered how they refused to take the kitten.

"Mom and Dad would just fight again," she said. "They'd never let me go."

We just sat there for a minute.

"Is your dad really going to spank you?" I asked.

"He usually forgets," she answered. "I don't think he really cares. It's just something to fight with Mom about. Dad isn't so bad, only he's gone so much of the time." She shifted and looked up at me through her hair. "You're so lucky! You aren't stuck with parents because you get to go to boarding school. Besides, your parents are halfway decent."

I swallowed and said, "Just remember, God really does love you."

"How come such bad things happen to me, then?" she demanded.

"I don't know. Because of other people's sins, I guess.

Mom says that sin always hurts. It hurts the people who do it and people around them, too."

"You mean, like Dad and Mom fighting hurts me?" she asked.

"I guess. I don't really get it all. I just know when I do something wrong, and I ask Jesus to forgive me, I feel way better inside. We had to learn this verse that says, 'The blood of Jesus Christ washes away all sin.'"

Tianna made a face, "That's gross. I don't want blood on me."

I laughed. "Not real blood, silly. Well, not exactly. See, sin causes pain and hurt and death. So if we sin, we should be punished, but Jesus loves us so much that he didn't want that. He let God punish him instead of us, and he even died for us. So it's like his blood kind of erases the sin off of us, because Jesus already paid for it." I paused. "We have to ask him to wash away our sins, though. He doesn't just do it to us. We have to decide to belong to him."

Tianna squirmed. "Come on, let's get out of here." She pulled my arm and headed for the back door.

"Wait a sec," I said. "I'll ask if I can go."

"You really are a goody-goody, aren't you?" she sneered, yanking on her jacket. "I'm going! If you want to come, come—but don't tell your parents. Or are you a tattletale, too? Come on!"

I just stood there trying to decide what to do. It was already dark out.

Tianna said, "Wimp!" and stuck out her tongue at me. Then she left, slamming the door.

Chapter Seven

I stared at the door, Tianna's angry words ringing in my ears. I frowned. Was I a wimp? I bit my lip and wondered where she was going. With a sigh, I went into my room to finish packing.

Later, Mom and Daddy came in to read the Bible with us. We did that every night. Most of the time Tianna had been coming, too.

"Where's Tianna, Anika?" Daddy asked.

I just shrugged without looking up. No matter what Tianna had said, I was no tattletale.

"I was looking forward to one last evening with her," Mom said. "She seems to be really interested in the things of God."

"Maybe she doesn't want to come tonight," I said. "She acted mad at supper."

Sandy had been teasing the kitten with a piece of shoestring as we talked. Now she blurted, "Please, can't we take Jake? He'll be sad without me, even if they do feed him."

Mom looked sad. "Sandy, you already know the answer to that. I'm a bit worried about Jake, too. How about if you pray for him?"

"Why pray for a kitten when Tianna is so upset?" I blurted. "People are more important."

Daddy nodded and said, "God cares for all the creatures he made, but you're right. We will certainly keep on praying for Tianna and her parents. I'm disappointed in how this visit has gone."

"It seems like we made it even worse for Tianna," I said.

"Why don't Uncle Kurt and Aunt Doreen just wise up!" Sandy said. "They're acting so awful."

"That's enough," said Daddy. He opened the Bible and started reading, "'When someone becomes a Christian, he becomes a brand new person inside. He is not the same anymore. A new life has begun! All these things are from God who brought us back to himself through what Christ Jesus did. And God has given us the privilege of urging everyone to come into his favor and be reconciled to him. . . . For God took the sinless Christ and poured into him our sins. Then, in exchange, he poured God's goodness into us!'"

I was half listening and half worrying about Tianna. What Daddy was reading said that we were supposed to

93

bring God's message of peace to people. We sure hadn't done very well with Tianna's family.

That night I couldn't go to sleep. No one had even noticed Tianna was out of the house. I wondered where she was and listened for her to get back. I could hear the low hum of the furnace. Car lights swept across the room now and then. Sandy was breathing with little snores. After a while Mom, Daddy, and Uncle Kurt went into the living room. I could hear them talking.

"Well, Doreen is working late again, and I told her to be here tonight," Uncle Kurt said. "I thought maybe you could talk some sense into her."

Mom answered, and I leaned up on one elbow to hear better. "You can't make people be what you want them to be against their will, Kurt. Even God doesn't do that."

"Well, she ought to listen to me!" Uncle Kurt's voice rose. Daddy's answer was low and quiet, so I slipped out of bed and pushed the door open to hear better. Maybe he'd say something to make Uncle Kurt see that God thinks women are people, too. What Aunt Doreen had said about Jesus having no women disciples still bothered me. With all the rush of getting ready to leave, I hadn't remembered to ask about it.

"Christian leadership isn't that way, Kurt," Daddy was saying. "Christ gave up his life for us. Ephesians 5 says that husbands are to love their wives in the same way. It says that husbands should love their wives as though they were a part of themselves."

"I thought you would be on my side," Uncle Kurt said, sounding hurt and angry. "I thought you'd help me uphold traditional values in this family. Do you think Doreen is behaving properly, then?"

Mom spoke up, and she sounded irritated. "Kurt," she said. "How Doreen behaves has nothing to do with you. Her problems don't excuse your behavior. Your so-called 'traditional' values are pure destructive selfishness. You just want to be in charge and get your own way. That's not Christian at all. The Bible says we are to submit first to Christ, then to one another. We are to consider others' interests more important than our own. The husband is to lead for the benefit of his family."

"So now I'm not Christian!" Uncle Kurt half yelled. "I don't need to listen to this."

I could hear his heavy footsteps cross the floor, then the front door slammed. I thought I heard Mom crying, but I couldn't be sure.

I went back to bed, but I lay awake for ages. Thoughts tumbled around in my head. Worry for Tianna was all mixed up with being happy about going home. Everything was just sliding into a dream about skiing when I finally heard Tianna come in and go to her room. I kind of wanted to get up and talk to her, but I was too sleepy.

I didn't see her again before we left, because our plane left really early, and she didn't get up.

Uncle Kurt drove us to the airport, but he would hardly even talk to Mom and Daddy. Sandy was crying about leaving her kitten. I felt strange—happy to be going home and to be getting out of that house, but sad and scared for Tianna. Aunt Doreen's question was also still bothering me.

On the plane all four of us ended up in a row in the center seats. I was next to Daddy. As soon as we were off, I blurted, "How come Jesus didn't have any women disciples?"

Daddy laughed and said, "I want your mother in on this one. Hazel, did you hear the question?"

He repeated it, and Sandy said, "You were listening to Aunt Doreen! She told me that, too, but *I* didn't listen."

I made a face at Sandy and said, "Well, I want to know. Why didn't Jesus pick any women? Aunt Doreen said the Bible says women aren't as good as men."

"Never believe that!" Daddy said firmly. "All over the world and all through history, Christianity has made men see women as equal with them before God. In pagan societies, men often use their greater physical strength to force their women into roles of virtual slavery. The Bible warns men to treat women gently, as fellow-heirs of the faith. What's more, the Bible tells us that God values us all just the same, regardless of whether we're male or female."

"Yes," Mom added, "and did you know that Jesus used women as the first witnesses of his resurrection? That could be considered the single most important event in human history, and he chose women to be his witnesses at a time when they could not legally testify in court. Besides, as far as disciples go, there was a band of women who traveled with Jesus through his whole time of ministry. In fact, they were the ones who provided for Christ and his disciples. There were well-known women of God in the early church, too, such as Priscilla and Phoebe."

"But—but . . . " I stammered, surprised at the force of their answers. "How come people get so upset about women being preachers now, then?"

"People disagree about that," Daddy said. "Some think women should be free to take any position in the church. Others feel that some positions were meant for men. The disagreement has nothing to do with whether women are as good as men. It has to do with the roles God intended each of us to play. Men and women are equally important, but they are different."

"I'm glad!" said Sandy. "I'm not the same as any dumb boy!"

We laughed, but Mom said, "That's not the heart of the problem, you know. The real problem is attitude. God wants every one of his children to look for ways to serve. Instead, we grab for power and status. That's Kurt's problem, as well. Oth of bem in that thamily are doing that."

We all grinned, and Mom looked frustrated for a second, then she laughed, too. I was still confused. It was hard to figure out all that stuff about different roles for men and women, and how one isn't better than the other. Even so, I felt better inside. One thing I did understand was that I was a person to Jesus. He didn't care if I was a boy or a girl; he loved me no matter what.

When we landed at Nairobi Airport and got off the plane, the rush of African sounds and smells made me grin. Spicy dust, hot sunlight, the smell of diesel fuel, the song of birds, the sound of Swahili, the wide savanna sky—all of this seemed to be welcoming me home to the continent where I belonged.

Back at the mission station, it was hard to think much about Tianna. The whole trip to Canada didn't seem real. In fact, everything about the Malcomes and their problems seemed far away and unimportant.

All the other kids were back at school, so the station

was really quiet. You see, most kids stayed at a boarding school in dorms for three months, then came home for one month. Sandy and I went to Valley Christian Academy boarding school because Mom and Daddy wanted us to have a good American education.

"Sandy and Anika, are you finished packing for school?" Mom said a couple of days later. "Daddy will be up here from the office in a minute, and we'll be ready to leave."

Just then, Daddy came up the hill from his office at a trot, waving something in his hand.

"Kevin, what on earth?" Mom asked. "What is it?"

"Anika, is this your doing?" Daddy demanded as soon as he got up to us.

I just looked at him with my mouth open. What did he mean? I hadn't done anything.

"This is a telegram from Kurt," Daddy said, waving it in my face. "It says Tianna will be here tomorrow."

"What?" I blurted. "Tianna here?"

"Yes. Kurt says that Tianna told him that we said she could come. Aunt Doreen left, and he has to go on a business trip, so he's sending her here."

"Doreen left?" Mom said. "Oh no!"

"Did you say that Tianna could come here?" Daddy asked again, staring straight at me.

I looked down.

"Well?" he demanded.

"She was so sad, so I said she could live with us," I said all in a rush. Then I paused and said, "I didn't think she'd ever really come. I mean, how could she without any money or anything?"

"What about Jake?" Sandy blurted.

"Never mind the kitten," Daddy said and turned to me again. "Don't ever do something like this again without talking to us first."

I hung my head and whispered, "Are you going to send her back?"

"Of course not," Mom said. "We can't turn her away. Besides, we don't want to. The last thing Tianna needs is more rejection. I only hope you're mature enough to be a help to her, Anika. This isn't going to be easy for any of us, especially you."

"What about school?" Sandy asked. "Are we still going today?"

Mom and Daddy looked at each other for a minute. Finally Daddy said, "I don't see why not. We'll have to decide what to do about Tianna's schooling when she gets here, but I don't see why either of you should miss another day."

"She wants to go to boarding school," I said slowly. The idea of having Tianna at Valley Christian Academy was gradually sinking in. I cringed inside.

"We'll have to see about that," Mom said. "Now let's get cracking. We want to get you there in time for supper."

Two hours later, Daddy drove down the hill toward my dorm. He was going to drop Sandy off last. I looked out the window anxiously. I could hardly wait to show Lisa my new Canadian clothes. Then I bit my lip. What if she already had other friends and didn't want me anymore? What about Muthoni and Amy? I'd kind of hung around with them last term. Would they remember me?

The car stopped, and I got out and stretched. Cool upland air, filled with the smell of cedar, surrounded me. I breathed deeply, and suddenly I was really excited to be back.

A bunch of kids came running out of the dorm. Lisa got to me first.

"Anika! Anika!" she yelled, running at me. "Mrs. Jackson said you were coming," she grabbed my arm. "I traded beds so you can have the bunk under me."

"How come y'all came back so soon?" Amy asked. Her parents are from Texas. Muthoni was right beside her. She had her hair done in these really neat cornrows.

It seemed like everyone was talking at once, so I couldn't even answer. I grinned and headed into the dorm.

Jackson dorm isn't really a dorm. It's a big house with two rooms at the back where all the fifth- and sixth-grade girls stay. Jacksons, the dorm parents, stay in the other end of the house.

Daddy, Mom, and Sandy helped haul my junk in. Of course, Mom said she'd be praying for me like she always says whenever they drop me off. There were quick hugs, and Mom and Daddy went to take Sandy to her dorm.

"Do you have any chow?" Amy asked.

"Whoever wants chow has to help me unpack," I said, grinning.

Chow is any food from home, and I had a whole batch of chocolate chip cookies.

"Hey! cool," Lisa said. She was holding up the big T-shirt I'd bought with Tianna.

It turned out that there weren't any drawers left for me. Sabrina Oats and Esther Miller had snitched the ones I was supposed to have.

"Come on, you guys. Get your junk out," I said.

"First come, first served," sneered Sabrina. She always was trouble for me.

"Don't be such jerks," Lisa said.

"Look who's talking," Esther said. "Little Miss Cool from California. You've got an extra drawer. Give her yours."

"Mrs. Jackson gave me that drawer," Lisa said. "Anika is supposed to have these drawers, and you know it."

I got mad and my cheeks got hot. It was like all my nervousness about being back at school and about Tianna rolled up and aimed itself at this hassle. Suddenly arguing seemed really stupid. I stamped over, jerked the first drawer out, and turned it over with a crash. My hands were shaking. I was just yanking the other drawer out when I realized the room had gone dead silent.

"Anika," a voice said from the door, "that wasn't necessary." It was Mrs. Jackson.

"But they wouldn't move their stuff," I blurted.

"I've had to speak to you about your temper before," she said, shaking her finger at me. "Apologize!"

"Sorry," I muttered.

"Now, who had things in the drawers I assigned to Anika?" she asked.

Nobody said a word.

She reached down, picked up a notebook, and read the name on the cover.

"Sabrina Oats, get your things back into your own space," she said. Then she turned to look at me. "Anika, I came in to welcome you back only to find you in a temper tantrum. You certainly don't make things easy on yourself."

"Look what time it is!" Muthoni said all of a sudden. We'd all missed the first supper bell.

"Run, girls, or you'll miss your supper," Mrs. Jackson said, making shooing motions with her hands. She's really not bad, just kind of bossy. I bolted out of there, still shaking from getting so mad.

We tore up the hill behind the dorm, through the black wattle trees, and across the gravel to the dining room. I tried to get away from the others. I was fighting not to cry.

"Stupid! Stupid! Stupid!" I hissed through my teeth as I ran. It seems like I should have learned that getting mad always makes things worse.

"Wow, you don't take long to make people mad at you," Lisa said as she skidded into the food line after me.

"Sabrina Oats always hated me anyway," I said, my voice low and sullen. "And Esther Miller always does anything Sabrina does." I looked down and twisted away from Lisa. I felt bad enough about dumping the stuff out. How come Lisa had to make it worse by talking to me about it? Why couldn't people just leave me alone?

"Hey, don't worry," she said. "I'm glad you're here."

I gave her a quick look and said, "Thanks." Then I realized she might be having her own problems, so I asked, "Is VCA as bad as you thought?"

She didn't answer because we had to go through the line. One of the servers slapped a huge glob of shepherd's pie on her plate.

"Not really," she said, then glanced at her plate. "Well, except for the food," she added, and we both laughed. "I still miss my friends from home, though." She wasn't laughing anymore.

The dining room seemed huge and noisy, like it always does the first day back at school. Lisa and I sat down, and Muthoni and Amy sat with us. I sighed with relief. At least they weren't mad at me.

Chapter Eight

~~~~~~~~~~~~~~~

After supper, I ran ahead and stopped where I could see down into the Rift Valley. Wind blew through my hair, lifting it right to the roots. I shook my head and laughed. VCA is high up—seven thousand feet above sea level—on the side of the longest valley in the world. Craggy volcanoes, Longanot and Suswa, rose out of the wide valley floor four thousand feet below where I stood. Everything was dusty gold from the evening sun. Nowhere in the world was more beautiful then here. I spread my arms and started leaping from rock to rock, daring myself to go faster and faster. I was a wild horse, I was a unicorn, I was free as the wind.

"Anika, wait up," Lisa called from the top of the hill. I stood still, completely still like a wild animal, and stared down into the valley. *How can anyone not believe in God when he makes things like this?* I wondered.

Lisa came running up, with Muthoni and Amy after her.

"You're weird, Anika," Lisa said, laughing.

I wanted to take off again. Being with people made me feel cramped and stuffy. But these were my friends, so I just stayed where I was.

"We'd better go back before Sabrina Oats messes up your stuff," Amy said. "Besides, you said we could have chow."

I nodded and took off running again. We all tore into the dorm panting and laughing. While we were unpacking my junk, I told them about Tianna. Afterward we all sat on the top bunk, eating chocolate chip cookies.

"You mean your cousin might be coming here?" Lisa demanded, reaching for a cookie.

"Yeah, Mom and Daddy might bring her after she's been in Kenya for a bit," I said. The idea of Tianna at VCA didn't seem real at all.

Muthoni had been biting her fingernails and looking worried. Now she said, "But she's not even a Christian. Why does she want to come here?"

"Tianna thinks her parents hate her," I answered. "She said boarding school sounded neat because you don't have to hassle with parents."

"So what if she's not a Christian?" Amy said, bouncing up and down a little. "Maybe she'll get to be one."

"I was waiting and waiting for you to come," Lisa interrupted, "and now you'll just hang around with your mixed-up cousin the whole time." She frowned and put down the cookie she'd been eating.

"I don't even know if she's coming for sure," I said desperately. Tianna wasn't even here and already she was wrecking things for me.

"Hey, I know," said Amy. "Let's pray. We can pray that if Tianna comes she'll get to be a Christian, and that we can still be friends."

"I don't know," I said slowly. "I thought that their whole family would get to be Christians when we went to stay with them, but it didn't work. Now her parents might even get divorced."

"I don't care," Amy said. "I'm going to pray about it."

She bowed her head and had just gotten started when Sabrina Oats barged in with Esther Miller following her.

"Anika Scott, you broke my china unicorn when you dumped my stuff," she yelled. "You'd better pay for it or else!"

"Shhhhh! We're praying!" Muthoni said.

Sabrina stopped for a second, then blurted, "So what? You're supposed to pay your debts first."

Esther Miller grabbed at her arm like she wanted Sabrina to back off. Sabrina shook Esther's hand off and said, "That unicorn cost thirty American dollars."

"That's ridiculous!" Lisa blurted. "Thirty bucks? That

little thing? No way. Besides, how do we know it's really broken, anyway?"

Sabrina whirled and grabbed what looked like a wad of Kleenex off her dresser. She spun back around and opened her hand in my face. The pieces of a delicate china unicorn lay there. Its head was beautiful. I reached out with one finger to touch it, feeling sad that it was broken.

Sabrina jerked her hand back. "You better pay up, Anika Scott, or else!"

She turned her back on us.

"Where am I supposed to get thirty bucks?" I whispered.

"She probably broke it herself," said Muthoni. "She's just trying to blame it on you."

"It never cost thirty bucks anyway," Lisa said.

I squirmed. I wasn't so sure. It was so pretty, and I *had* dumped her stuff. Just then Mrs. Jackson called us for devotions. I shoved thoughts about the unicorn out of my head.

During the next few days I got back into the routine of boarding school. Lisa, Muthoni, Sabrina Oats, Esther Miller, and I all were in one room. Amy was in the other room with different kids, but she spent most of the time in our room. I didn't even think about Tianna. Sabrina Oats kept hassling me about the unicorn. I ignored her.

"Let's make a fort," Amy said on the way down from breakfast that Saturday.

"Yeah!" Muthoni said. "Like that one we had last year, only better."

"There's a really good clump of trees behind that big rock," I said, pointing.

"No, I mean down below the dorm," Amy said. "Come on!" She took off running, with Muthoni after her. I started, then looked back. Lisa was still walking. Muthoni and Amy had been best friends for ages. They'd let me hang around with them, but I'd never really had a best friend 'til Lisa came.

"Hurry up!" I called. Lisa didn't move any faster, so finally I stopped to wait. "What's wrong?"

"Forts are little kid stuff," she said.

"Oh, come on," I blurted. "I love forts."

She did come with me, but she still wouldn't run. When we were almost there, I ran ahead.

Muthoni and Amy were in a really thick clump of small black wattle trees. Even though the smooth, gray bark and feathery leaves of the wattle trees didn't scratch, I could hardly push through because the trees were so thick. They were way too close together to grow properly.

Amy had found a spot in the clump where you could stand up.

"OK," she said, "This will be the middle. We can bend those ones down and tie them."

"Shh!" said Muthoni, making frantic 'come-here' motions with her hands. "I've got a great idea," she whispered. "If we're really quiet, the other kids won't even know we have a fort."

Amy giggled. "Sabrina Oats won't be able to bug us here. I'll go out and make sure nobody can see us. You guys start working, but be quiet."

A second later I was going in circles twisting off a tree with a trunk about as thick as my big toe. The little tree was growing in the middle of what would be the fort floor. Muthoni was hacking at another one with a stone.

"Nobody can even tell we're here," Amy whispered, grinning, as she came back to join us. She picked up the tree I'd finally twisted off and started stripping the bark. It came off in long tough strings from bottom to top.

"Lisa, you're taller," she said. "Help me hold this, OK?"

We bent down the taller trees and tied their tops together with bark strips. Pretty soon we were in a sort of upside-down basket made of little live trees that were tied together at the top. Our fort was big enough to stand up in and even walk around a little.

Lisa, who had mostly been watching, suddenly said, "Hey, this is cool! We never had forts anything like this in California."

"Shhhh!" hissed Muthoni.

"Sorry," Lisa whispered. "But look, if we make the door a sort of tunnel, then it will look like a big igloo."

She crawled out the little space we'd left as a door and started tying the teeny-weeny trees that were clumped there at the top to make a tunnel.

"Neat," I whispered, crawling after her. "We can make it a secret entrance so even if the other kids find the fort they can't get in.

By midafternoon we had the fort almost done.

"Up there," Amy said, lying on her back on the floor of the fort. "I can see sky."

"Here?" asked Muthoni from the outside. We were weaving little branches though the holes. If we did it right, the rain wouldn't even get in.

"No, further down."

I put my hand in one spot and said, "Is this it?"

"Yeah," Amy said.

I poked my leafy little branch through. The end was in my face, all cool and tickly, and I was trying to get hold of the stick and fish it back through.

"Anika! Anika Scott!" That was Mrs. Jackson. We all stopped and listened.

"I saw them coming down this way, Mrs. Jackson." That was Esther Miller's voice. They were coming toward us.

"Drop!" hissed Amy.

We all fell on our stomachs and held absolutely still.

If I answered Mrs. Jackson now, I'd give away where the fort was. I could hear their feet coming closer.

"Anika! Anika Scott!" yelled Mrs. Jackson, so close that I jumped. Fortunately, they didn't hear me, and soon their footsteps got fainter.

Amy made shooing motions at me. I nodded and crawled out toward the opposite side of the clump of bushes from where Mrs. Jackson had gone. As soon as I was out I ran in a loop, up the hill and back around.

"Did you call me, Mrs. Jackson?" I said, panting as I ran up to her from the opposite direction of the fort.

"There you are, Anika," she said. "Your folks are here looking for you."

Without waiting to hear the rest I took off for the dorm with a huge grin on my face. At the top of the hill I almost knocked Mom down. She caught me and hugged me. I squeezed her tight. It was so great to be up tight against the smell and feel of my own mother. It wasn't like I'd been homesick or anything, but it was good to see her.

Daddy hugged me, too, and his rough cheek

scratched mine when he gave me a kiss. I let go and looked at them, and realized Tianna was behind them.

"Uh, hi, Tianna," I said. It was weird to see her. It felt like one of those pictures where little kids are supposed to find the thing that doesn't belong. Tianna's head was down and she was looking at me through her bangs. Her hair was brushed and in a barrette, though.

"How did you get so dirty?" she asked.

I frowned and looked down at myself. Making a fort never was a clean job. Then a sick sort of *zing* went right through me. What would happen about the fort now that Tianna was here? Would we have to let her in? Maybe the rest of the kids would kick me out because of her.

"Ummm . . . " I said and paused.

Mom broke in. "You can talk later," she said. "Let's go get Tianna settled in."

"You're staying?" I asked Tianna. I'd been hoping Mom and Daddy had just brought her up to see what VCA was like. At least that would give me some time to get used to the idea of Tianna being there with me. It hadn't seemed real before.

"Yeah, I'm staying," Tianna said and glared at me like she was daring me to say something. I looked away. After all, I *had* told her to come.

"Hazel," Daddy said, "I'll go drop off some things and

talk to Glen Bishop. I should be back in about half an hour. Anika, come get a hug in case I miss you later."

In the middle of the hug, he whispered, "I'm counting on you to do your best with Tianna. We're behind you all the way, and we'll be praying for both of you."

He gave me a grin, gently bopped me on the top of my head with his fist, and left.

We started up toward the dorm, and Mrs. Jackson came over and said, "I moved Lisa to the other room so your cousin can have the bunk above you."

I looked at her in horror. Mrs. Jackson smiled and patted my shoulder. "It's nice to have a chance to let cousins be together," she said. "I'll just go finish moving Lisa's things."

I dropped back beside Mom, who was a little way behind Tianna, and whispered, "Mom! Lisa traded beds so we could share bunks. Mrs. Jackson never even asked her about this."

Tianna looked back and Mom shushed me.

"Mom, please," I whispered. "I've got to go and warn Lisa or she's going to think I did it."

"Anika, that's enough fussing," Mom said. "The first priority is making Tianna feel welcome."

Yeah, right, I thought angrily as I fell into step beside her. I had to make Tianna feel welcome while she was trashing my life.

In the dorm we started putting Tianna's stuff into Lisa's drawers. Mrs. Jackson and Mom were talking at her about how much she was going to like it at VCA, also about the rules and stuff. As usual with grown-ups, Tianna wasn't saying much. She kept looking at me, kind of hopeful and worried.

I felt sorry for her, but I had to warn Lisa. "Excuse me a minute," I said and headed toward the bathroom. You can see the door out of the dorm from our room, so I yanked open the window above the tub and climbed out. A second later I was running full tilt toward our new fort.

"Tianna's here!" I panted as everybody stared at me after I came tearing in. "It's not my fault, Lisa, really it's not."

"What's not?" Amy demanded.

"Mrs. Jackson gave Tianna Lisa's bed," I answered, then I looked at Lisa. "Mrs. Jackson has moved all your stuff into the other room already."

There was a stunned silence, then Amy said, "Maybe we'll end up sharing bunks, Lisa."

"I've got to get back. I had to sneak out to warn you," I said, turning to crawl out of the fort. "Please believe me, Lisa. It wasn't my idea," I said over my shoulder.

She just looked at me without saying anything.

I said, "Please?" one more time, then turned and ran back to the dorm.

By the time I got back, Mrs. Jackson had gone. Sabrina Oats and Esther Mills were sitting on their beds staring at Mom and Tianna as they unpacked.

"There you are, Anika," Mom said and looked at me hard. "I'm going to walk up to Sandy's dorm so I can see her before she leaves for supper. Your dad will know where I've gone."

I nodded. Mom gave Tianna a hug, but Tianna stood stiff as a stick, so she let go and said, "Remember we'll be praying for you, Tianna. We really do care."

Tianna gave one jerky nod and turned back to the drawer she was arranging.

Then Mom reached for me. While she was hugging me she whispered, "You know we pray for you all the time. I think you wanted to help Tianna by inviting her to come. It won't be easy, but she needs your friendship. Look up Galatians, chapter six, and read the first few verses, OK? You can do it."

She gave me another squeeze and left.

I took a deep breath, looked at Tianna, then thought, *OK, I will be her friend. I won't cop out.*

"Do you want some chow?" I asked Tianna.

"Some what?" she asked, turning around.

Sabrina Oats and Esther Mills laughed, and Tianna

whirled on them. "I don't know who you two think you are, but where I come from it's not polite to stare or eavesdrop."

"This is our room, too," Sabrina said. "What are we supposed to do, put our heads under the pillow so we can't hear you?"

"Come on, Tianna, let's get out of here," I said. "It's almost suppertime anyway."

Suddenly I could think of a hundred things I wanted to ask her.

"What happened?" I asked as soon as we were out the door. "I mean, how come you got to come?"

She shrugged and looked away from me. Then she said, "You know, you really conned me. So far Kenya is the pits."

"It is not!" I half yelled.

"It is," she said, yanking out the barrette in her hair and marching across the yard. "That mission station where your parents live is the world's most boring place! No TV, no mall, no nothing. They took me down some stinky little red dirt track covered with cow pies to see these men hacking at hunks of wood."

"I like watching the carvers at Mavivia," I said loudly, following her.

She sat down on the edge of the hill behind a bush so no one could see us from the dorm and kept right on talking. "And this place, so far it looks like some second-rate Bible camp. That woman—what's her name?—Mrs. Jackstoned? All she talked about was rules. You actually like this place?"

"Why don't you just go home then?" I said, jumping to my feet and facing her. "You didn't *have* to come here!"

Suddenly she put her head down on her knees and started sobbing. I stood looking at her for a second, then sat down beside her. I hugged my knees and looked at her out of the corner of my eye, wondering what on earth to do.

"I did!" she said between sobs. "I did have to come. Mom left without even saying good-bye, and Dad didn't want me either."

She sobbed even harder. "He said it was because he had to go up north on a job, but that was just an excuse."

"How did he know you could come here?" I asked. "I never told him."

She drew two big whooping breaths and looked up at me. "I asked him," she said, and ducked her head and started crying hard again. "But I didn't want him to say yes."

I shifted uneasily. My seat was beginning to feel cold because the grass was damp. I tried to imagine what it would be like for my parents not to want me.

"Um," I said, "I want you, Tianna," and tried to swallow the guilty, not-wanting-her feelings.

She lifted her head and glared at me through red puffy eyes. "You think I'm stupid?" she demanded. "I heard what you said about me making your friend move."

"I do want you. I promise," I said. "I decided when Mom was talking to me that I will be your friend, no matter what."

She stared at me for a second, like she was trying to decide if she believed me.

"Tianna! Tianna!" somebody yelled. I looked up. Sandy was running across the yard toward us at full tilt.

"What happened to my kitten?" she said, panting, as soon as she was close enough.

Tianna looked away, and I said, "Leave her alone."

"What happened to Jake?" Sandy yelled. "I came right after supper. I'm out of bounds to come here, but I had to know."

Tianna didn't look up. Before I could stop her, Sandy grabbed Tianna's shoulder and shook her, yelling, "What happened to Jake? What did you do to him?"

I shoved Sandy back, and she hit me. I got mad and shoved her as hard as I could. She fell down but got right back up.

"Stop it!" Tianna said. "I don't know. Jake was still

there when I left. Dad said he would take him back out to Parkers', but he doesn't always do what he says."

"Leave her alone!" I said to Sandy. "Can't you see she's crying?"

"Oh," said Sandy. She looked like she was going to cry, too. Something inside me twisted, and I wanted to keep Sandy safe. I wished I hadn't pushed her. She said "Oh" again, then whirled and ran off.

"Sorry for pushing you," I yelled after her. She didn't even slow down.

Then it sank in. She said she came after supper. Tianna and I had missed supper. Well, at least we still had chow from home.

"Come on, Tianna, let's go in and get some chow," I said.

She just shook her head without looking up at me.

"I'll bring you some, then," I said and headed for the dorm.

Chapter Nine

I was standing staring at the note I'd found in the cookie crumbs on the bottom of my empty chow tin when Lisa walked in.

"Look at this!" I hissed, waving the note in Lisa's face. I felt hot from head to foot, and the paper shook in my hand.

Lisa took the note out of my hand and read it out loud: "'This chow has been taken as part of the payment for my unicorn. Hope it doesn't poison me. Sabrina Oats.'"

"Those turkeys!" she yelled. "That's stealing! Amy! Muthoni! Look at this!"

"I bet she knew we missed supper, too," I said. "Did she take Tianna's?"

Tianna's box was empty, too. Her note said, "The Bible says we should take care of our relatives. You just helped pay for my unicorn, which your cousin broke."

I slowly shut Tianna's chow tin and put it back. Amy, Muthoni, Lisa, and I just stood there staring at each other for a second. Then Lisa said, "I'm going to get Mrs. Jackson."

"That's telling!" Amy called after her.

"I don't care," Lisa called back.

We looked at each other uneasily. "Well, you don't have to go hungry, anyway," Muthoni finally said. "We snuck you some food."

She reached into her pocket and brought out a couple of hunks of bread with a piece of gooey meat in between. "Here," she said, handing it to me.

Amy took more bread and meat out of her pocket. "It's for Tianna," she said. "We prayed and decided to even let her into the fort."

Lisa, Muthoni, and Amy deciding to be nice to Tianna was the only good part of that whole evening. Tianna took one look at the gooey meat and bread they'd snuck out of the dining room for her and pitched it down the hill. Mrs. Jackson yelled at Sabrina Oats and told her to give the chow back. She said she'd eaten all of it. Ha!

We couldn't get Tianna to come in the dorm until Mr. Jackson practically marched her in for devotions. I forgot to tell her about her missing chow before we went to sleep that night.

Crash!

I sat bolt upright in bed.

Crash!

The noise had come from the bathroom. It was the middle of the night and pitch dark. Somebody started swearing at the top of her lungs.

"Tianna?" I asked. It was her! "Tianna!" I yelled and started climbing out of bed.

Sabrina screamed and then yelled, "Stop it! Let go of my blankets!"

There was a thud, and Tianna hollered, "You thief! You'll find out you don't mess around with me!"

I started across the floor toward the light and tripped over something soft and lumpy. I was trying to get up when the light came on.

Muthoni was by the switch, blinking. Sabrina and Tianna were tangled on the floor in a blanket, hitting at each other.

I grabbed Tianna and tried to pull her away. Sabrina's nose was bleeding.

"What is going on here?" a deep male voice said. Mr. Jackson was standing there in his housecoat, glaring at us.

"She attacked me!" Sabrina yelled, pointing at Tianna. "She swore out loud and attacked me for no reason." Sabrina wiped at her face with her hand and then stared at the blood and started howling.

"No reason?!" yelled Tianna. "This creep stole my food!"

"I'll deal with these two," Mr. Jackson said, taking a

step forward and grabbing both Sabrina and Tianna by the arm. "The rest of you clean up this mess and get back to bed."

Mr. Jackson left, taking Tianna and Sabrina with him. We stared at each other wide-eyed for a second. Everybody from both rooms was there. Then Amy went over and picked up one end of Sabrina's mattress, which was on the floor, and said, "Come on, you guys. Help."

Esther Miller grabbed the other end, and we got busy cleaning up.

Muthoni found Tianna's chow tin on the floor. One side was all dented in. She picked it up, turned it over, and said, "I bet she got up and took this into the bathroom because she was hungry. Then she found the note and got mad."

"Did she ever!" I said.

Just then Mr. Jackson marched Tianna and Sabrina back in. "Tianna," he said, "this kind of behavior is completely unacceptable here, no matter what the provocation. Is that clear?"

Tianna nodded and gave Sabrina a dirty look through her bangs.

Mr. Jackson stood and watched until everyone was in bed, then said, "For Pete's sake, get back to sleep!" and left, slamming the door.

"That man washed out my mouth for swearing!" hissed Tianna. "I'll kill him!"

"Shhh!" half the people in the room shushed. I lay in the dark, as stiff as a board, wishing I was back home with Mom and Daddy.

For breakfast the next morning we had birdseed. Well, it was really hot cereal, but it looked like birdseed, so that's what we called it. I like it. It's bumpy and warm in your mouth and tastes kind of like nuts.

Tianna picked up a spoonful and let it drip off in little globs. Then she did it again, lifting her spoon even higher.

"This stuff is gross!" she said, blobbing her spoon up and down on the top of her cereal. "I can't believe you're eating it."

Lisa giggled. "That's what I thought, too," she said, taking a bite from her bowl. "Actually, it's not as bad as it looks. It's better than glue or fingernails."

"They feed you glue and fingernails?" Tianna said in a squeak.

We laughed, and I said, "Wait and see."

Tianna had made me late for breakfast. She wouldn't get out of bed, and when she finally did she just pulled some clothes on and didn't brush her hair. It was a good thing I'd read Galatians 6:2 like Mom had suggested, otherwise I probably would have just left.

The first verse of the chapter had been talking about what to do when somebody else was being bad. It said we should gently try to help them do right. Then it said, "Share each other's troubles and problems, and so obey our Lord's command."

"Come on, Tianna, brush your hair," I had said. "Your mom can't see you here, and it's Sunday."

"Mind your own business," she had snapped and headed for the door.

Lisa, Muthoni, and Amy had saved us a place at their table, so it could have been worse.

After breakfast we walked up to Sunday school. The sun was shining, and I looked up at the dark green hill high above us. The bright edge of a white cloud showed above the top of the hill. It was so pretty against the deep blue sky. I spun and walked backwards to look at the valley. The wind blew the ends of my now-short hair into my face.

Amy giggled. "This wind makes me feel like I have no hair."

I laughed and shook my head so my hair flew around. "My hair's like a horse's mane," I said, running and picking my feet up really high like I was trotting.

"Race you to the fig tree," Muthoni yelled, and took

off at a dead run. I quit trotting and tore after her. Her thin brown legs flashed, and she beat me by two steps.

Muthoni and I were still laughing and breathing hard when we went in to Sunday school. Lisa, Tianna, and Amy came in a couple seconds later when we were already singing, "Praise the Name of Jesus." I liked that song and I sang with all my might. "He's my rock . . ." My hands stung from the clapping. "He's my fortress, he's my deliverer, in him will I trust. . . . "

I remembered how God had kept Lisa and me safe several months before. We'd been swimming in the ocean and had gotten caught in Mida Creek, a very strong current that can grab you and carry you away from shore before you even know it. We'd been carried pretty far—I could still remember how scared we were. But God had been watching over us, and we made it to shore, and back home, safely.

I looked over at Lisa, and she saw me and grinned. Then I looked at Tianna. She was just standing there with her mouth shut. For a minute I thought she was just being mean. Then it hit me that she probably didn't know any of the songs.

As soon as the song was over, Miss Garrett stood up to teach. She's a bossy old lady with legs that look like cigars. Once she gave Darren Brown a demerit for chewing gum.

"We have a new student in our class this morning," she said, "but before I introduce her, I'm going to ask her to go and brush her hair." There was a shocked silence, and I slid way down in my seat. Nobody moved.

"Well," said Miss Garrett, glaring at Tianna. "Are you intending to be insubordinate as well as sloppy? At VCA we don't come to Sunday school with our hair looking like a rat's nest."

A couple of boys giggled. Tianna got up and bolted from the room. She didn't come back.

Miss Garrett cornered me right after class. "You realize," she said, leaning over me, her perfume nearly smothering me, "that I meant no harm. Your cousin must understand we have standards of behavior here."

I squirmed and jerked my head in a nod. I had to get out of there and find Tianna.

"That's fine, then," Miss Garrett said, patting my shoulder. "You'll tell her for me. I won't report her for missing Sunday school."

I nodded again and ran.

Lisa, Muthoni, and Amy were waiting for me in a little knot on the porch.

"I've got to find Tianna," I said, pushing past them.

"I know," said Amy. "We'll help. We were just waiting for you. Muthoni and I will search around here. Lisa, you look beside the path and stuff."

"I'll go to the dorm," I said and took off, then stopped to yank off my Sunday shoes and socks so I could run faster. The *slap, slap* my bare feet made on the packed dirt of the path sounded loud as I ran downhill.

"Looking for a rat's nest?" Sabrina Oats called as I tore by her and some other kids. Their laughter followed me as I ran.

Tianna was sitting on her bed, stuffing things into a gym bag. "I'm getting out of here," she said as soon as I walked in.

"Miss Garrett said to tell you she was sorry," I said. *Well, she did, sort of,* I told myself. Besides, I had to calm Tianna down.

"Everybody hates me," she half yelled. "Mr. Jackson washed my mouth out with soap. They feed me glop and humiliate me, and that Sabrina Oats geek stole my food." She glared at me. "So tell me why I should stay."

"Lisa, Muthoni, and Amy don't hate you," I said. "They're trying to be your friends. So am I. And Jesus loves you, too. Besides, where would you go?"

There was a long pause, then she said, "I guess you're right." She shrugged and looked down. After a second she looked up, shook her hair out of her eyes, and almost yelled, "I'm telling you right now, if it doesn't get better, I'll find a way to get out of here!" She looked at me for a second, then frowned. "You wouldn't tell me how to get out of here even if you knew, would you?"

"I don't really know, anyway," I said, looking away from her. I didn't, not exactly. "Besides, if you tried to fit in a little it wouldn't be so bad here. All you need to do is brush your hair, and don't swear, and clean up when we're supposed to, and junk."

"Don't you bug me, too," she said and walked out. She went and sat at the edge of the yard and looked down over the valley.

When I followed her, she said, "Leave me alone, OK?"

"You sure you're all right?" I asked.

She nodded and looked straight ahead, so I left her. Back inside I looked at her messy bed. The part of the verse that said, "Help each other with your troubles," ran through my mind.

OK, Jesus, I'll try. Then I started to make Tianna's bed.

Tianna came back in just as I was finishing. She gave me a funny look, then went over and got her brush out. She stood there holding it, not brushing her hair.

Sabrina Oats walked in. "Hi, Rat's Nest," she said. "I know, I'll just call you Rat for short. Bitten anyone lately?"

"I told you last night not to hassle me," Tianna said,

swinging around to face Sabrina. "I meant it, ditz brain."

"*Tsk, tsk,*" said Sabrina. "The beast is becoming enraged."

Esther Miller interrupted. "Sabrina, don't. It's not funny."

My mouth fell open. Esther Miller was standing up to Sabrina Oats! Sabrina whirled on her. "Stay out of this," she said, her voice low and mean.

"Sabrina," Esther said, "don't bug her, please."

"What's the matter, you afraid of her? Well, I'm not afraid of that," Sabrina said, jerking her head toward Tianna.

"I'm not scared," said Esther. "It's just that we're supposed to be Christians and she isn't and she's here all by herself." Esther said it all in a rush, with her shoulders hunched and her head down.

Sabrina flushed and ducked her head. Then she blurted, "I thought you were my friend," and left the room.

"Thanks, Esther," I said.

Esther gave me a nervous smile, then said, "I've got to find Sabrina."

"'We're Christians and she isn't'," said Tianna in a singsong voice. "If Sabrina Oats is a Christian, she can keep it."

I squirmed. "It's not like that. I mean, being a Christian doesn't mean you're perfect all of a sudden. It means, like, you want to belong to Jesus, and he loves you and forgives you and helps you do the right thing."

"Like Sabrina Oats making fun of me?" Tianna demanded, yanking the brush though her hair.

"No," I said, "like Esther standing up for you, or Lisa deciding to be your friend even after you took her bed—"

"*I* didn't do that," Tianna interrupted.

"I know, it was Mrs. Jackson. But if you decided to be a Christian . . . " I stopped and swallowed hard, watching Tianna to see if she'd be mad.

She stopped brushing her hair and said, "Well?"

"If you did, it wouldn't mean you'd never do dumb things. But you would know that Jesus is taking care of you, and that makes things OK when you're lonely and your mom and daddy are so far away, or when people make fun of you, or when you do something wrong or just really stupid. Jesus helps you change."

"I wish he'd hurry up with Sabrina Oats, then," she said and jerked the brush savagely through her hair. She threw the brush down and shook her head so her bangs were back in her face. "Come on," she said. "It must be almost lunchtime. Let's go try the glue, or is it fingernails this time?"

I laughed and said, "No, those are for breakfast. Maybe they'll give us garbage patties for lunch."

She gave me such a horrified look that it made me laugh even harder. On the way up the hill, we met Muthoni and Amy coming down. "You found her!" said Amy.

"I couldn't believe Miss Garrett," said Muthoni.

"You're from here, aren't you?" Tianna interrupted, looking at Muthoni.

"No, from Nairobi," Muthoni said.

"Well, if you wanted to get out of here, would you know how?"

I shook my head at Muthoni, but she didn't see me. She just gave Tianna a funny look and said, "Take a matatu up and catch a bus at Kishengo."

"What's a matatum, or whatever?" asked Tianna, "and where do you get one?"

"It's a truck, and you catch them down by the hospital," Muthoni said. Then she stopped, put her hands on her hips, and demanded, "Why are you asking me these things?"

"No reason," said Tianna and ran ahead.

Things seemed to go better after that. Tianna even brushed her hair, made her bed, and got to breakfast on time the next day. Monday afternoon we finished the fort, and Tianna actually seemed to like it.

Then everything fell apart at recess on Tuesday.

I was sitting at my desk finishing some math corrections that Mr. George said we had to get done before we could go out. I looked out the window at the sunshine on the top of the wild olive tree below our classroom and then back at my paper. I erased a wrong answer and tried to think. I could hear kids out on the porch, laughing and running.

A voice outside rose to a yell, and a couple of other voices joined it. I held still and listened.

"Rat's Nest is chicken! Rat's Nest is chicken!" a couple of boys' voices chanted.

I stood up to see out the window better. Trevor Norton shoved Tianna toward the big rope swing that was hanging from a branch of the wild olive tree. Tianna whirled and slugged him hard in the stomach.

She swore at the group, then yelled, "Mind your own business."

I ran for the door.

"Careful! Rat bites!" I heard Sabrina Oats yell. "Rabid rat bites."

I got outside just as Tianna ran at Sabrina and shoved her hard. Sabrina went backward, down the hill, and started screaming—a high, different scream than when she had been teasing Tianna.

A scream that didn't quit.

Chapter Ten

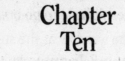

I reached the edge of the hill and looked down. Sabrina was still screaming. She was lying on her side, partway down the hill. Mr. George came running and bent down over Sabrina, who moaned, "My arm! My arm!"

The kids were in a big circle all around. Tianna, her hair over her face and her big blue eyes full of fear, looked down the hill at Mr. George and Sabrina. I went toward her, and Mr. George looked up and saw me.

"Anika, go get the nurse," he said. "I think Sabrina's broken her arm."

I paused and looked at Tianna—she looked so scared—but Mr. George said, "Hurry, Anika! Run!"

By the time I got back—the nurse had brought me with her in the car—the other kids were back in the classrooms. Mr. George helped to put Sabrina in the car and left with her for the hospital.

In our classroom the kids were all in clumps talking.

"Well, I don't think she's so bad," Amy was saying. "I

mean, how would you feel if your parents separated and sent you to the other side of the world?"

"So?" said Trevor. "She doesn't have to go breaking people's arms."

I looked around frantically, but Tianna wasn't there. "Where is she?" I asked Lisa quietly.

Lisa shrugged and said, "She took off right after you left." The classroom door slammed into the wall as I tore out of the room. What if Tianna was running away? What if she was already gone? I raced down the hill, my breath tearing in my throat and my lungs hurting.

I shot into the dorm room and skidded to a stop. Tianna wasn't there. Her drawers were hanging open. I yanked the closet open and looked inside. Tianna's gym bag was gone. I whirled and ran out of there toward the hospital.

Darn that Muthoni! I thought furiously between breaths. My side hurt, so I dropped into a walk. Suddenly the song we'd sung on Sunday came into my head, "He's my rock, he's my fortress, he's my deliverer, in him will I trust. Praise the name of Jesus."

It was like a weight went off me. I took a slower, deep breath and said, "OK, Jesus, you're my safety. Let this be your thing. I can't handle it. I don't get why you let this happen, but help me be on your side. You handle it."

Suddenly I wondered if I was all worried for nothing. Tianna probably didn't have any money, so she couldn't go anywhere. She'd be scared and mad, though. I started trotting again.

There are always quite a few people around at the kiosk by the hospital. There were women sitting on the ground, bright scarves on their heads. A bunch of people were sitting on rickety chairs outside a little shop, holding glasses full of strong milky tea. A matatu, which is like a small pickup truck with a covered back, was there, and people were crowding around to get on. A boy wearing ragged khaki shorts ran up to me and said, "Givi me a money!"

One of the African ladies yelled at him in Kikuyu, and he looked at her and ran off. I searched the group frantically, looking for Tianna. Then I saw a white face in the back of the matatu. It was Tianna! The matatu started to drive away.

I ran after it, waving my arms and yelling in Swahili, *"Bado! Bado qua mimi!"* Wait! Stop! Stop!

There are lots of different languages in Kenya. The people around VCA talk Kikuyu. Other tribes talk Kikamba or Masai. White people talk English, Danish, French, or whatever, and Indian people talk Hindi or Urdu. But the one language that all the different groups speak is Swahili. It's called a trade language, which means everyone uses it to talk together. The only people who talk Swahili at home are the Swahili, and they live at the coast. Many Kenyans speak three languages: their tribal language, Swahili, and some English, which they learn in school. Like most kids on the mission compound, I knew enough Swahili to get by.

The driver of the matatu heard me yelling and stopped. I ran up and grabbed hold of the tailgate. "Tianna! Come on, get out. You can't—"

The matatu started moving. The driver couldn't see me from the front and must have thought I'd gotten on. I couldn't just leave Tianna. I held on to the side and jumped on the bumper. Two African men in the back grabbed my arms and helped haul me on board. I whacked my knee hard on the tailgate.

"Eeeea, *pole pole,*" a bunch of the people said almost in chorus. *Pole pole* means something between "I'm sorry" and "Take it easy."

I staggered forward, trying to keep my balance. People squashed over to leave room, and I sat down hard by Tianna. The shoulder of the man next to me was practically in my ear. The back of the tiny pickup was packed. Everybody was staring at us.

"Tianna, we have to get off!" I blurted, trying to stand up. "Kids who run away get expelled from school."

She jerked me down. "No way."

I landed with a thud and looked back at the road disappearing behind us. We were headed for the big highway above the station.

"You can't keep running away. I don't have any money, and I bet you don't either," I said. "The driver will be really mad."

"No, he won't," Tianna said. "I told him that all I have is American dollars. Dad gave me a bunch when I left. He said they're good anywhere in the world. The driver of this taxi thing took them, anyway. He took ten bucks and said he'd take me to some hotel at Naibashi or somewhere. I'll pay for you, too. I'm not going back now. He was really helpful."

I bet, I thought. That driver wouldn't want to let us off, not if he thought he'd lose a chance at getting more American money. He could change the dollars on the black market for an awful lot of shillings.

"Did he say Naivasha?" I asked Tianna. She just shrugged, so I looked up and asked, "Is this matatu going to Naivasha?"

A couple of people shrugged, but a girl whose whole head was covered with tiny long black braids so that she looked like an Egyptian princess answered in English. "The driver has told her that he would deliver her to the tourist hotel near the lake at Naivasha. Your friend showed him many dollars, so he will be happy to take you, too."

A wave of fear went over me. If people knew Tianna was carrying a lot of money, we could get robbed.

Just then the matatu jerked to a stop. We were at Kishengo, up by the highway above the station. People started climbing out. I got up, too, but Tianna jerked me down again.

I grabbed the girl's sleeve and started talking Swahili so Tianna wouldn't stop me. "Please, can you get someone to tell the people at VCA where we have gone?"

The girl nodded as she climbed over the tailgate.

"What did you say to her?" Tianna demanded.

I shrugged.

"I bet you're trying to get me caught," she said. "You're no friend!"

"OK, let me go back, then," I said. She was still holding on to my arm. The driver was outside yelling out where we were going, and new people were crowding into the matatu.

Tianna clutched my arm tighter and stared at me, wide-eyed. "No, I'm scared."

I swallowed and thought, *I'm scared, too.* The matatu started moving, and I was nearly squashed when the fat lady next to me lurched into me.

My jaws snapped together when the matatu hit an

extra big pothole. The bones in my seat already hurt from being whacked by the hard ledge we were sitting on.

If this matatu takes us to the hotel at Naivasha, I thought, *I can call home from there. I could if I had some money anyway.*

"Tianna," I whispered, turning my head and putting my mouth close to her ear. "How much money do you have?"

She shoved me off with her elbow. "Stop it!" she demanded loudly. "Don't hiss in my ear. It's not a state secret. I've got two hundred bucks."

"Shhh!" I hissed furiously. "You don't have to brag. That's more than most Kenyans ever see. We're just two kids by ourselves, so shut up about it, OK?"

Her hand flew to her mouth and her eyes opened wide. "I showed the driver," she said in a scared whisper.

I frowned without answering and slid lower on the ledge, hugging my arms. Just last term two of the seventh-grade girls went off campus by themselves, and a man had threatened them and yanked their watches off.

The matatu jerked to a stop. It was hot inside and stunk of sweat from crowded people. I looked out but couldn't tell where we were. A woman with three tiny kids climbed on. People scooted over and she sat down right across from us. The toddler pressed himself up against his mother's leg, put his thumb in his mouth, and stared at us with huge dark eyes. His little brown shoulder showed through a huge hole in his ragged T-shirt.

Suddenly Tianna and her whole family seemed like spoiled brats to me. There they were, rolling in money and luxury, and all they could do was make trouble for themselves, while people like that cute toddler's mom were struggling just to feed their kids and send them to school. It wasn't fair! I wanted to grab Tianna's money and hand it to that woman.

I glanced at Tianna and sighed. She was looking out the back and chewing her fingernails. She probably would make a big stink if I grabbed her money. Besides, if I gave the money away, what would happen to us?

"Chicken," I whispered at myself. The matatu started again with a jerk that banged my back against the hard edge of the truck. I watched the road going backwards, and the people walking on the side getting smaller, and wished I'd never met Tianna. My stomach felt hollow and scared. On top of that, it was lunchtime and I was hungry.

We stopped at Naivasha town by the shops, which are called *dukas*. Everybody started climbing off.

"Come on," I said to Tianna and got up to follow.

"Is this where the hotel is?" she asked.

I barely nodded. It wasn't, but I wanted to get away from that driver who knew about Tianna's money.

We were the last people in the matatu, and I'd just started climbing over the tailgate when the driver saw me.

He hurried toward us, shaking his head and flapping his hands at us. "I have said I will drive you to the hotel. I will truly drive you to that place. *Karibu.* Sit, sit."

Karibu means "Welcome" or "Come in." Without pausing, he rushed around to the cab.

"Hurry, Tianna," I said, one leg over the tailgate.

"The hotel isn't here, is it?" she demanded.

"Come on!" I said and reached back to grab her arm.

It's a good thing I did, too, or I would have been thrown out when the matatu shot forward. Instead, we both fell onto the floor.

"Ow!" Tianna yelled, getting up off of me and holding her head. "You geek! Why did you grab me like that!"

I got off the gritty, rattling floor of the matatu and glared at her. "Me?" I said furiously. "How about you? Did it ever occur to you that that man might hurt us for your money?"

I sat down with a thump on the opposite side of the matatu from Tianna.

"If you wanted to get off to get away from the driver, why didn't you say so instead of trying to make me think it was the stop for the hotel?" she said, frowning.

The knot in my stomach tightened. I hadn't exactly lied, but I hadn't told the truth either, and now things were worse.

"Sorry," I muttered.

There was a long silence. I tried to remember the way to the hotel from Naivasha, but I'd only been there a couple of times. The road unwinding behind the matatu didn't look familiar. A wave of goosebumps went over me in spite of the heat, and tears stung my eyes.

Finally Tianna said, "If you're such a good Christian and really believe that stuff, maybe you should ask God to take care of you." Then she added in a small voice, "And me, too."

I looked up at her in surprise. She was right. I hadn't asked God to keep us safe.

"OK," I said. "Good idea." Then I bowed my head and prayed, "Dear God, please keep us safe. Help Mom and Daddy or people from VCA to find us soon. Also, I'm sorry I lied to Tianna when I wanted her to get off this matatu. Um . . . please help the driver not to hurt us or steal Tianna's money, and help Tianna to get to know you. In Jesus' name, amen."

Immediately I felt much much better inside. My stomach didn't even hurt so much.

"Do you think he heard you?" Tianna asked.

I nodded.

"Then I wish you didn't ask him to let people from VCA find us," she muttered, shuffling her feet on the gravelly floor. "They hate me."

"They do not!" I said. I looked anxiously out the back, then had to brace my feet to keep from being knocked off the seat by another big bump. We were off the pavement, and dust was pouring into the back. Where was this matatu taking us? I swallowed hard. "Tianna, remember that song we sang at Sunday school? Can we sing it now?"

"I didn't know any of those songs," she said, scooting away from the back of the matatu to get out of the thickest dust. "Yuk! I hate dust."

"Well, I want to sing it," I said and started. At first my voice came out all quavery—only partly because of the bumpy road—but by the end of the song I was singing out. I knew Jesus really was my safety.

"Come on, you sing, too," I said to Tianna.

"Praise the name of Jesus! Praise the name of Jesus! He's my rock, he's my fortress, he's my deliverer, in him will I trust. Praise the name of Jesus!"

Tianna sort of joined in, then shook her head. "Anika, he's not my rock and all that stuff. I'm scared!"

"Do you want him to be?" I asked.

She nodded. "Ever since I watched your whole family praying at my house, I kind of wanted to do that, too. I was just scared God only liked good people like you guys." She looked up at me, and tears were running down her dusty face. She sniffed hard.

In fourth grade the teacher had made us memorize ten verses that she called the way of salvation. It had been kind of a pain. I mean, I knew all that stuff. But now a verse popped into my head to answer Tianna.

"No, God loves bad people, too," I said, leaning forward and touching her knee. "The Bible says that 'God showed his great love for us by sending Christ to die for us while we were still sinners.' See, God does love you. You can just ask him, and he'll be your rock, too."

Tianna looked at me hopefully across the bumping, dusty matatu.

"You have to say you're sorry, and ask Jesus to forgive you, and all that," I blurted.

"OK," she said, nodding, and then just sat there looking down.

I looked apprehensively out the back. The driver might stop any minute. There was nobody to help. I shifted uneasily and said, "Come on, hurry up before something happens."

"What do I do?" she asked.

"Just talk to Jesus," I said. "He's always listening."

There was a long, dusty, bumpy pause, and I bit my tongue to keep from telling her to hurry again.

"Um, Jesus," she finally said. "Anika said you love me. Can I please belong to you like she does? I'm sorry for being such a jerk. Please love me. Um, I guess I'm supposed to end by saying amen, so amen." She looked up at me. So much of her dusty hair was in her face I could hardly see her. Then she shoved her hair back and grinned.

"He heard me. He did! I just know it!"

I grinned back, so big that it made my cheeks ache, and started singing again. "Praise the name of Jesus . . . " Tianna joined in really loud. "He's my rock! He's my fortress! He's my deliverer! In him will I trust!"

The matatu jerked to a stop. We stopped singing and looked at each other, then I looked out the back. I could see level grass, flower beds, big acacia trees, and lawn chairs. "We're at the hotel!" I said and started climbing out.

The driver hadn't taken us somewhere else to beat us up and steal our money. Even so, I was still nervous about facing him. He came to the back and reached to help Tianna out. She ignored his hand and climbed out on her own. Pulling her gym bag with her, she stood behind me.

"I have brought you as I had said," he said, looking at Tianna, "and also I have brought your sister with you."

"OK, I'll pay you for her, too." She turned her back on

him and hunched over her gym bag to open it. I guess she was trying not to let him see. She shoved something into my hand and said, "Here, give him this."

It was a ten-dollar bill. I held it out, and he took it with both hands, kind of bowing. *"Asante.* Thank you, thank you," he said and gave us a big smile.

He climbed back into the cab of the matatu, then leaned out. "My mother also is a Christian, and she has sung that song that you were singing. Your God has kept you safe." He gave an emphatic nod and said, *"Aya, Quahairi,"* and drove off.

A wave of relief washed over me.

"What did he mean by that?" Tianna asked.

"I don't know," I said, staring after him. "Anyway, we're safe. God kept us safe!"

I grabbed Tianna's hands and started dancing around. She grinned. I let go and did a cartwheel.

"Come on!" I yelled, bouncing onto my feet again. "Let's go call Mom and Daddy."

I ran for the hotel.

"Wait, Anika!" yelled Tianna, running after me. I slowed down and she grabbed my arm, her eyes full of fear. "Please, Anika. Don't call anyone. At least not until tomorrow. Let's just stay here tonight."

Chapter
Eleven

I stared at Tianna and let her words sink in. She wanted us to stay, by ourselves, at the hotel overnight. She also wanted me not to tell Mom and Daddy. And she had all the money.

"I have to call them," I blurted. "They'll be really worried. Besides, I don't think the hotel will let us stay here, just two kids with no grown-ups." I looked at her curiously. "Why do you want to stay here, anyway?"

She looked away from me, then rubbed a hand across her mouth. "I'm kind of scared to go back," she said. "I don't really know your mom and dad that well, and the people at VCA . . . " She hunched her shoulders and hugged herself. "I mean, I'll go back, really I will—but I just want time to get used to being a Christian."

I looked at the hotel. I'd been here before with Mom and Daddy. We hadn't stayed overnight or anything, but it didn't seem scary. It might even be kind of fun staying in a fancy tourist hotel by ourselves. And Tianna did have enough money.

Anyway, I thought, *if that girl in the matatu tells someone where we are, like I asked her to, people from VCA might already be on their way to find us.*

"Um," I said trying to decide. "Um, if I agree, can I call Mom and Daddy and tell them?"

"They'll just come get us and take me back to VCA," Tianna said. Her face was dusty and streaked with tears. She really did look scared.

"I'll tell them not to come 'til tomorrow," I said, shaking her hand off impatiently. Why did she have to be so silly? "Look, if you don't let me call, I'll tell the people at the hotel we're runaways. What if the hotel doesn't let us stay by ourselves, anyway?"

"OK," she said. "Call your parents, then."

"Great! Come on!" I yelled and took off for the lobby again. Tianna followed me in so slowly that I had to wait for her by the hotel desk for ages.

The man looked at us oddly, but he let us book a room after he saw Tianna's money. They changed a bunch of it for her into shillings, too. I actually got through to Daddy's office my first try, which hardly ever happens with Kenyan phones.

"Anika! What's happened?" he said, sounding alarmed. We're not allowed to call home unless there is an emergency.

"Um, I'm at the hotel at Naivasha," I said.

"What!?"

"Didn't VCA call you?" I asked.

When he said no, I told him what had happened and ended with, "The best part is, Tianna's a Christian now, too."

"Well!" he said and paused. "We'll be there as soon as we can. I'm just glad God kept you both safe. That's good news about Tianna."

"Look, Daddy, Tianna doesn't want to go back yet. She wants to stay here tonight. She had money, and we already checked in. I promised you wouldn't make us go back tonight."

He chuckled. "You did, did you? OK, we won't make you leave tonight. But we're not going to leave you there alone, either. I'll call VCA to let them know where you are."

My stomach tightened again at the thought of being in trouble at VCA, and I blurted, "Tell them I didn't run away on purpose."

"I'll talk to them," he promised. "And then we'll come to stay with you."

I hung up with a sigh of relief. No matter what Tianna said, I was glad Mom and Daddy were coming. Now staying here could be fun.

Tianna was staring at me.

"They said we could stay," I told her, grinning.

"All right!" she yelled before I could finish. "Let's go get something to eat."

"Maybe we'd better wash up first," I said, looking at her filthy face. I didn't really want to tell her Mom and Daddy were coming. Even if she was a Christian, she might run away again or something.

After we were cleaner we headed for the restaurant. Tianna must have stayed in hotels with her parents before, because she knew exactly what to do, how to order and stuff. It felt odd not having someone else in charge of us. It was fun, too.

We walked down to the dock by the lake after our late lunch. Beautiful big yellow-barked acacia trees were all around. Hundreds of birds were singing and flying back and forth through the flat feathery-leaved tree-tops. Sun shone on the blue water, and huge water lilies floated by the dock. Cormorants sat on a twisted, black, dead tree that stuck out of the lake a little way from shore.

I shut my eyes and turned my face into the warm sunlight. Everything was going to be all right. I remembered a picnic our whole family had had here once, and how Daddy took us all for a boat ride afterwards.

"Your family want to rent a boat, please?" a man said right beside me, like he'd been reading my thoughts.

I'd just turned to look at him when Tianna said,

"Look, Anika, that man by the hotel. Isn't that Mr. Jackson?"

I spun and looked. It *was* Mr. Jackson. He was heading for the lobby. He hadn't seen us.

"I'm getting out of here," Tianna said and ran down the dock. An Indian family was just climbing out of one of the boats. The little outboard motor was still running. Tianna grabbed the rope from the father, climbed in, and took off.

I stared after her with my mouth open. Where did she learn to run a boat so well? I looked back up at the hotel but couldn't see Mr. Jackson anymore. I swiveled frantically and looked at Tianna's boat going out through the shining blue water. We'd never find her if she got away. And I remembered Daddy saying Lake Naivasha could be dangerous. It didn't look bad right by the shore, but the wind could come up suddenly. I also knew that the edges of a lake where hippos and crocodiles lived could be dangerous.

"Stop her!" I blurted to the man. "We have to stop her!"

He was staring after her, too, and his eyes were wide open, looking very white in his dark face.

"Ndiyo! Yes!" he said, *"Yeye ni mtoto tu."* Which means, "She's only a child."

He climbed into another boat and yanked the rope to

start the engine. I jumped in after him so fast that I almost tipped the boat over. The boats looked like aluminum rowboats with little outboard engines bolted to the stern.

A second later we were putting across the water after Tianna. The outboard motor smoked and sputtered. I looked up. Tianna wasn't getting any farther ahead, but we weren't getting any closer either. She looked back and saw us.

"*Haraka! Haraka!*" I said, hitting the side of the boat like it was a horse. *Haraka* means "hurry."

"There is not petrol in that boat," the boatman said complacently in Swahili.

Suddenly Tianna turned her boat and headed for an overgrown stretch of shoreline. Her boat putted into a narrow channel through the reeds—and disappeared.

The boatman slowed down almost to a stop.

"*Hii ni njia ya kiboko,*" he said.

A hippo path! Tianna had headed down a hippo path. No wonder the man didn't want to follow her. We hear of people who are killed by hippos every year. Most people don't think of hippos as being dangerous, but if you get in their path when they're going into the water or leaving it, sometimes they just bite you in half. True, it was daytime and hippos mostly come out of the water at night . . . but still!

I stared, paralyzed, down the channel through the reeds where Tianna had disappeared. I shivered.

"Come on, we have to help her!" I insisted. *"Twende!"*

The boatman shrugged and put the boat back in gear. We chugged slowly down the channel. Reeds that were taller than a man stood up on both sides of the boat. I held the edges of the boat so hard that the metal pinched into my fingers. It was hard to hear anything but the motor. Tianna's boat finally came into view. She wasn't in it! I almost choked, picturing her already knocked into the water and dead. Then the boatman pointed to her tracks heading up the bank.

The shore was a hard bank of mud about ten feet wide. Paths went off from it into the thick bush. Hippo paths.

"Tianna!" I yelled, like her name had been torn out of my throat. "Tianna, come back! You'll get killed! These are hippo paths!"

I listened, but all I heard was a bottle bird making its *blup-blup, blup-blup* call, sounding like someone emptying a bottle. I couldn't see anything. We were totally hemmed in by reeds and bush. The stifling hot air smelled like rotting mud.

Just then something splashed behind us in the rushes. I jumped and looked back. Hippo? Nervously, the boatman was looking behind us, too.

"Tianna!" I yelled frantically. "Tianna!"

A terrified scream split the air, then there was a loud slithering splash and the sound of something big going through the rushes to our right. There was crashing in the bushes, too. I jumped so hard that the boat rocked, which made me grip the edges even tighter. Was Tianna dead? Did a hippo get her?

The crashing in the bush came closer, and then Tianna came tearing through the bush off the path and hurled herself at our boat. She hit the boat, one foot in and one foot out. She was going so fast that she went straight over the far side. There was a loud double splash. The boat pitched and bucked under me, and I gripped the edge even harder. Tianna came up screaming and lunged at the side of the boat. It pitched sideways and nearly went over, then steadied.

"Pole pole!" the boatman yelled from near my elbow. That's when I realized he'd been dumped out when Tianna hit the boat. His wet black hands on the gunnel were steadying the boat now.

Tianna lunged into the boat, landed at my feet with a thump, and screamed, "Crocodile! Crocodile!" pointing shakily back the way she'd come. Then she started a whooping, screaming cry.

"Alikwenda,"—he has gone—said the boatman, pushing the boat to the edge, where he climbed in.

"Tianna!" I yelled at her and shook her. "Tianna! It's

OK. The crocodile left as fast as you did. We heard it go through the rushes."

She suddenly clutched my legs and hugged them hard. I could feel her body shaking with her sobs. I didn't know what to do, so I just sat there.

The boatman got hold of the rope from the other boat, and we started chugging back through the reeds. I peered anxiously ahead, afraid we'd meet a hippo coming in. When we chugged back out into the wide, glittering blue water of the open lake, I sighed with relief. Tianna wasn't shaking so much, but she was still clutching so hard that her arms were hurting my legs. I was just going to ask her if she was OK when the boatman made a hissing noise.

I looked back at him, and he was pointing. The glossy dark brown top of a hippo's head was showing just above the water about twenty feet away, watching us. Another set of bumpy nostrils and eyes came up beside the first one with a loud, steamy snort. The second hippo stared at us, waggling its little pinky-brown ears to get the water out.

I held my breath as we putted slowly away from them, but they didn't do anything. Tianna never even saw them. Usually we always point out any animals we see so everyone gets to see, but somehow I didn't think Tianna would appreciate it just then.

I looked back at the hippos, then toward the dock. Ducks flew off the water in front of us, and water lilies brushed the side of the boat. A cool breeze lifted my bangs, and the glitter from the water sparkled in my eyes. I breathed more easily.

Tianna finally let go of my legs and sat beside me.

"You OK now?" I asked.

She nodded. "I thought that path through the reeds was a place where people had taken boats out. I thought I could leave the boat and walk to a village or something and just come back when your parents come tomorrow. I mean, I can drive boats. Dad lets me drive our waterskiing boat at the lake sometimes."

"It was a hippo path," I said.

"Yeah, I heard you yell. And I was just starting back toward the lake on a different path when there was this huge crocodile right in front of me. It was enormous and it stood up like a triceratops."

She shivered against my arm.

"They rest by the edge of the water," I said. "Did it chase you?"

"Yes!" she said, then paused. "Actually, I don't know. Next thing I remember is seeing you and this African man in a boat and me hitting the water. I was sure there was another one in the water, and I'd be eaten. It was awful!"

She shook even harder and started crying again. I wished Mom and Daddy were there.

Mr. Jackson was waiting on the dock. Tianna was still shaking so hard that he and the boatman had to practically lift her out.

As soon as they let go of her, she shied away from Mr. Jackson.

"I didn't mean to break her arm," Tianna blurted to Mr. Jackson. "Really, I didn't mean to break Sabrina's arm."

"Let's get you back to school and clean you up," he said. "We can talk about this later—"

"No!" I broke in. "Mom and Daddy are coming. I called them." I felt odd and shaky.

"I guess we'll have to stay and wait for them," he said, not sounding very pleased.

"They're not coming until tomorrow," Tianna said, hugging herself like she was cold.

"No, I didn't tell you . . . " I started, then it hit me— maybe Tianna wouldn't have run from Mr. Jackson if she'd known Mom and Daddy were coming today. When would I ever learn to tell the whole truth? "They said they would come and we all could stay here tonight," I said. "They're on their way now."

Then I noticed the boatman waiting. We hadn't

thanked him or paid him for using the boats or anything.

"Asante! Asante sana!" I said to him, which means "Thank you very much."

Mr. Jackson was pulling out his wallet when Tianna suddenly said, "I can pay him."

She stuffed her hand into her soaking wet pocket, and blurted, "Hey! My money's gone!" She paused. "I had it when I was down by the dock. It must have fallen out by the crocodile."

"By the *crocodile?*" asked Mr. Jackson, turning from paying the boatman.

"I'm *not* going back there. The crocodile can keep it," said Tianna, and we all laughed.

The boatman had seen Tianna come up empty-handed, and I didn't think that the money would be lost long. *Good,* I thought. *I hope he finds all of that money. He's a nice man.*

"I have to hear this story," Mr. Jackson said, looking at us, his eyebrows raised. "But first, Tianna, you go into the hotel washroom and clean up. I can't afford to have you getting sick. There are parasites in that water that are at least as bad as crocodiles."

His eyebrows went up again when I told him we had already booked a hotel room.

"What parasites?" Tianna demanded as she shucked off her wet clothes in our hotel room.

"Bilharzia or something, and amoeba, and stuff," I said. "They're like little worms that get into you from the water and make you sick."

"Gross!" Tianna screeched and ran for the bathtub.

Chapter Twelve

When we came out of the room after Tianna was all cleaned up, Mom and Daddy were standing talking to Mr. Jackson. I ran to them.

Mom hugged me especially hard and said, "I'm slo gad you're safe."

I giggled and said, "Me, too."

Tianna was walking toward us slowly, looking scared. She hadn't brushed her hair after she washed it so it was all over the place. Mom reached for her to give her a hug. Tianna tried to dodge, but Mom hugged her anyway.

"Tianna," Daddy said, "I've been talking to Mr. Jackson, and we need to have a talk with you."

She looked down. I squirmed and thought, *Why can't they leave her alone?* Then I blurted, "She's a Christian now!"

"That's a big decision. Are you sure you've decided to belong to Christ, Tianna?" Daddy asked, sounding serious.

Tianna gave a jerky nod, her head still down.

"You realize that you'll have to stop running away?"

Tianna nodded again.

"Aunt Hazel and I feel it would be best if you went back to VCA and faced any trouble you've made for yourself there. Mr. Jackson will take you back to VCA."

"Daddy," I said, "everybody's going to stare at us and ask us questions. Can't we just go home for a couple of days?"

"Better to face consequences sooner than later," said Mom. "But at least we can eat supper before you go. Mr. Jackson, would you like to join us for a picnic supper?"

After supper Daddy wanted us to pray together. He started, "Dear heavenly Father, I'm so glad you brought Tianna into your family with us. . . ." While he was praying for Tianna to have courage to face her problems, I opened my eyes, then squinted at the shaft of low sunlight that shone in my face. I turned my head and saw that the light was painting the big acacia tree trunks bright gold. Long shadows lay across the lawn. I smiled. God's beauty was shining right on me.

When we left, Tianna hugged Mom and Daddy back when they hugged her. She was very quiet on the way to VCA. Mr. Jackson wanted to know about what had happened, so since Tianna didn't answer, I had to tell him.

"Tianna," he said gently when I got to the part in the

matatu when Tianna asked Jesus into her heart. "I hope you didn't do this just to make us more lenient with you, or—"

"No!" she interrupted. "I wanted to! With Jesus I'm not all on my own anymore." Then she added, glaring at him through her messy mop of hair, "I'm tired of having everybody against me."

"Hey, I'm not against you," he protested. "I think it's been you against me and just about everybody else, even yourself. You've just about convinced me that you've made a real commitment to Christ, so things should be changing now. We'll have to let the other kids know, too." He smiled at her and reached out to knuckle her head. She ducked away from him and eyed him warily.

When we got back, Mr. Jackson called a dorm meeting. All the fifth- and sixth-grade girls crowded into the Jacksons' living room. Sabrina was there with her wrist in a cast.

"Girls," Mr. Jackson said, "Tianna and Anika have something to say to you. Tianna wants to apologize, and she has some good news to tell you. Stand up, girls."

I gasped. At least he could have warned us. Tianna looked totally panicked. I was afraid she was going to run again, but she just pushed at me to go first.

I stood up. "Um," I said and paused. It was dead quiet and everybody was staring at me. This was even worse than I had thought it would be. "Um, I just want to tell you that Tianna is a Christian now, and, um, I'm just glad God brought us back safe."

"Is running away a good idea?" Mr. Jackson quizzed.

"No!" I said, then added defiantly, "but it helped Tianna get to be a Christian."

Mr. Jackson frowned and said, "Tianna?"

"I'm through with running away," she answered fiercely. "It only makes things worse. Also, I'm through with fighting and swearing. Oh, and I'm sorry Sabrina's arm got broken." She looked straight at Sabrina and added, "I didn't mean to do that, but I don't think it was all my fault. There, is that what you wanted me to say?" she said, looking at Mr. Jackson.

He raised one eyebrow, but he said, "That will do. I have talked to Sabrina as well, and I agree, she's got some changing to do also. Right, Sabrina?" he asked, looking at her. Sabrina glared and looked away.

Mr. Jackson kept on talking. "Girls, I want all of you to help Tianna with this. It isn't always quick or easy when Jesus changes your life. I don't want any more heckling or mocking going on. Is that clear?" He said the last sentence really fierce, looking straight at

Sabrina. She turned red and looked down. Then he read the end of the fifth chapter of Matthew.

"Jesus is talking here, and he says, 'Love your enemies! Pray for those who persecute you! In that way you will be acting as true sons of your Father in heaven. . . . If you are friendly only to your friends, how are you different from anyone else? Even the heathen do that. But you are to be perfect, even as your Father in heaven is perfect.'" When Mr. Jackson finished reading, he looked around the room and said, "I expect to see that attitude shown here."

As soon as the meeting was over, most of the kids crowded around us and started asking questions.

"Enough!" shouted Mr. Jackson. "There's school tomorrow. Get to bed."

Amy, Muthoni, and Lisa just kept asking questions, following us to our room. We all ended up at the sinks brushing our teeth together. They seemed so happy to see us that Tianna was even starting to smile.

"Mmmf, I'm glad youw a Chishian now, Tianna," Amy said through a mouthful of toothpaste.

"Me, too!" said Muthoni, rinsing her toothbrush under the tap. "That was neat the way it happened in the matatu and how God kept you safe. The way I got to be a Christian was really boring compared to that." She sighed sadly, and we all giggled.

"OK, you five, enough talking. Get into bed," said Mrs. Jackson as she walked into the bathroom. We grabbed our toothbrushes and scattered to our rooms.

"Shhh!" Esther Miller said to Sabrina as Tianna and I came in.

"I don't care if she hears!" Sabrina said, half crying. "My arm really hurts, and it's all Tianna's fault!" She glared at us. "Besides, you still owe me for the unicorn, Anika. I'll get—"

Mrs. Jackson walked in just then. "Sabrina, I've brought you more medicine to keep your arm from hurting." I guess she saw Sabrina was crying, because she sat down on the bed beside her and put her arm around her. "I'm sorry it hurts so much. If it gets too bad in the night, call me."

While she was talking, Tianna leaned down from the top bunk and whispered, "That part Mr. Jackson read about what Jesus said, is that right?"

I nodded, and she asked, "Did Jesus even mean being kind to jerks like Sabrina Oats?"

I nodded again, and Tianna pulled her head back up when Mrs. Jackson turned out the light. I started to try to think how what Jesus said fit what I should do about the broken unicorn, but I went to sleep instead.

In the middle of the night the bunk bed jiggled hard, and I heard moaning. I sat up quietly. In the square of moonlight shining through the window, I could see Tianna walking across the room.

"Sabrina," she whispered, "are you OK?"

Sabrina stopped moaning.

"Do you want me to get Mrs. Jackson?"

"Leave me alone!" Sabrina hissed fiercely. "It's all your fault. I hate you!" She pulled her blankets over her head.

"Look, I said I'm sorry." Tianna's voice was getting louder like she was getting mad. "You ditz brain, you can just—" Then she stopped. With a sigh she said, "I guess I'm not very good at acting like one of God's kids yet, you know, being kind to your enemies and all that. I'll just leave you alone if that's what you want."

I felt ashamed. Tianna had only been a Christian less than a day and here she was trying to be nice to Sabrina. I hadn't tried even once. I climbed out of bed and bumped into Tianna as she came toward me to go climb back in bed.

I pulled her with me toward Sabrina, whispering in her ear, "Way to go. That was great." Then I said louder to Sabrina, "Look, I'm really sorry I broke your unicorn. Maybe I can get my parents to lend me the money to pay for it. I didn't ask yet."

I stood there for a second waiting for an answer, but Sabrina didn't move. Finally I said, "Um, you were moaning, so your wrist must hurt. We'll get Mrs. Jackson. Come on, Tianna."

Mrs. Jackson came, and we went back to bed. Just before I went to sleep, I asked God to help me learn to be nice to Sabrina. It was a big request, but I figured he could do it. All I had to do was go along with it. . . .

After breakfast, on the way up to school, Amy and Muthoni got Tianna between them. "Hey, I heard you last night talking to Sabrina. She didn't even answer!"

Tianna shrugged.

They kept talking, and I ended up walking behind them with Lisa. She grinned at me and said, "Welcome back, O Crocodile Woman."

I laughed and shoved her. She shoved back. We were both giggling, and I felt great. Lisa was super.

Just then Esther Miller came tearing up. She stopped a little ways off.

"Anika, Tianna, come here," she said, hanging back.

I looked at Lisa, shrugged, and followed Tianna over.

"Look, Sabrina said to say she was sorry for being so mean," Esther said and looked back over her shoulder. Then she went on, "She even said that you don't have to pay for the unicorn. Um, look, I'm sorry about taking one of your drawers, too. OK?"

"OK," I said. Tianna nodded, and Esther ran off

again. We looked at each other and grinned. This was turning out to be a great day.

That night I couldn't go to sleep. I kept thinking about that broken unicorn. I squirmed, then punched at my pillow to make it more comfortable. I could still see the unicorn in my mind, its delicate beauty lying broken in Sabrina's hand. I wondered if it really cost as much as she had said. What if Sabrina had been lying?

I rolled over with a jerk. The bunk bed squeaked and wiggled. My sheets were all tangled up.

"Hold still!" Tianna hissed.

I frowned and tried to hold still. A lump in the sheet was right under my shoulder blade. Sabrina had *said* I didn't have to pay her. Besides, I didn't have thirty bucks. Still, it bugged me. Finally I decided to write to Mom and Daddy and ask them what to do. I went to sleep trying to plan the letter.

Writing that letter wasn't easy, especially when it came to telling Mom and Daddy about how I'd lost my temper. I felt way better when it was done and mailed, though.

"What *is* this stuff?" Tianna asked, poking her spoon into the thick gray porridge in her bowl that Friday at breakfast.

"Glue," said Lisa, laughing.

Tianna made a face. "Let's go to McDonald's and get an Egg McMuffin, OK?"

"Don't I wish!" said Lisa with a dreamy look on her face. "I'd get hash browns, an English muffin, and—"

"Stop it! I can't stand it!" Tianna said and started to shake all over. "I'm going into terminal McDonald's withdrawal."

We were still giggling by the time we got to school. We were just starting social studies when the secretary stuck her head in the door. "Could you send Tianna and Anika out?" she said. "There's someone here to see them."

We looked at each other, then stood up and went out. I couldn't figure out who could want to see just us two in the middle of a school day. We reached the office, then stood staring in amazement.

"Dad?" said Tianna.

It was Uncle Kurt!

He took a big step toward Tianna and gave her a huge hug, then grabbed her by the shoulders. He seemed all choked up and started talking real fast. "Tianna, I'm sorry—sorry for all the ways I've messed things up. I didn't know how much I needed you 'til I got back from my trip to an empty house. It was awful—too quiet and lonely. Look, your mom won't come back to me—but I hope maybe you will."

She stood there, looking kind of stiff, staring at him with her mouth open.

"Oh, I know it hasn't been great lately, but things will be different. I promise. I called Kevin and Hazel from the airport and found out you were here, so I rented a car and came straight here."

"Uncle Kurt," I interrupted. "Tianna is a Christian now."

Uncle Kurt glanced at me, then looked back at Tianna, "That's OK with me. You can go to church. I'll even come with you if that's what you want. I never knew how much I needed my family until I didn't have you with me."

She still just stood there, so he said, "I did some thinking about what Kevin said, too. So look, I won't make you come. You can decide for yourself. Kevin and Hazel already said you could stay here. Go on with you, back into class. I'll drive down to see Kevin and Hazel, and you can let me know tomorrow."

Tianna was quiet all the rest of the day.

"What do you think she'll decide?" Lisa asked me when we were walking to the dorm after supper.

I shrugged. "I don't know. Would you go back now if you could?"

"If Mom and Dad did? Sure!" she said and laughed. "Big Macs, here I come!"

I looked out at the huge sweep of sky over the volcanoes in the Rift Valley and said, "You're crazy!"

Mom and Daddy came up with Uncle Kurt the next day. They took Sandy and me and Tianna down to Thompsons' farm for a picnic. They'd even brought samosas. I bit into one of the spicy little triangles and thought, *Who needs McDonald's?*

I was just going to ask Mom if they'd gotten my letter about Sabrina's unicorn when she handed me the money.

"Your father and I agreed that you should pay for what you broke," she said. "You'll have to work for us to earn this money next vacation, OK?"

I nodded and started to say OK when Tianna suddenly blurted, "I decided."

We all looked at her.

"I'm going home with Dad." She looked at me anxiously and said, "It's not that I don't like you guys. It's just that I belong with Dad, and if I stayed here it would be kind of running away."

Everybody immediately started talking about plans, packing, and tickets.

"Kurt," Mom interrupted after a little while. "I hope you'll find a good church and go with Tianna."

"I intend to do just that, but I'm not sure where," he said seriously.

"Call John Ibbotson," Mom said. "He pastors a warm and friendly church where they teach God's Word."

Uncle Kurt looked thoughtful, nodded, then got up to call the airport about flights.

Mom turned to Tianna and said, "Tianna, if you want to survive as God's child, you have to stick with God's family. Even if your dad doesn't take you to church, you can go on your own. It would be good for you to try to find Christian friends at school, too."

Tianna nodded, and I wondered what it would be like for her. I thought of Sharra, and how Tianna skipped school to go to the mall, and how she had spent so much time being sent to the principal for swearing. I wondered if Uncle Kurt had really changed or if he would start acting selfish and super bossy again. I sighed. It wasn't going to be easy for them, that was for sure.

Uncle Kurt found out they had to either get a flight out that night or wait for two weeks.

"You better get packed if you're coming!" he told Tianna with a grin.

"Uncle Kurt," Sandy said as we hurried to finish the picnic. "Did you really take Jake back to the Parkers'?"

"Jake?" Uncle Kurt asked, sounding puzzled. Then he said, "Oh, you mean the kitten. Yeah, I took him back. Don't worry, he's fine." He turned to Tianna and said, "We can go get him back again if you want."

Tianna grinned and started to nod, but then she frowned. "He probably wouldn't like being my kitten. He didn't like me much before, and he'd have to be all by himself in the house so much." She looked really sad.

Mom touched her shoulder and said, "Why don't you ask the Parkers for two kittens? That way they'd have each other to play with all day. And they'll learn to trust you if you show them you care by how you act."

Uncle Kurt chuckled and said, "Kind of like being a parent, isn't it? Do you think we can handle it, Tianna?"

Tianna grinned and hugged him. My eyes felt kind of teary. It was the first time I'd ever seen her hug her dad.

We cut the picnic short and went back to VCA to pack up Tianna's junk.

"Are you going to be really OK now?" I asked her when we were by ourselves for a second.

She shrugged and said, "Better than before. Like, then I thought nobody wanted me at all. Now I know that Dad really wants me. I mean, he came all the way to Africa to get me. And you guys want me. But the best part is that God wants me."

"Hey, you don't even have a Bible, do you? Except that one Mrs. Jackson lent you." I grabbed mine from the dresser and shoved it into her bag. "Here, only you have to read it. Promise?"

She laughed, "OK, I promise."

A few minutes later Sandy and I and half of the kids in Jackson dorm were waving at Tianna, her dad, and my parents as they pulled out. Tianna's hair was all messy and in her eyes as she turned to wave.

But she was smiling.